IZHIMA

KIRENAI FATED MATES

TAMSIN LEY

Twin Leaf Press

All characters in this book, be they supernatural, human, or something else entirely, are the product of the author's imagination. Any resemblance to actual people, situations, or events are entirely coincidental.

No part of this book may be reproduced, transmitted, or distributed in any form or by any means without explicit written permission from the author, with the exception of brief quotes for use in reviews, articles, or blogs. This book is licensed for your enjoyment only. Thank you a million zillion hearts and kisses for purchasing.

Cover by The Book Brander

Paperback version
ISBN-13: 978-1-950027-67-5
Copyright © 2022 Twin Leaf Press
All rights reserved.

Twin Leaf Press
PO Box 672255
Chugiak, AK 99567

Dear reader,

Be sure to check out the glossary at the back if you are into that sort of thing. Plus there is a bonus section with descriptions of the alien races you may encounter in this series. Happy reading!

XOXO

Tamsin

1

IZHIMA

I look with dismay at the long list of recipes for "gluten-free birthday cake" listed in the database from Earth's world wide web. When the cruise director asked me to make one, I assumed "gluten-free" was a flavor and that I'd be able to find a recipe easily. I am a renowned Nebula Chef, after all, and I've earned stars in eight other culinary styles. But apparently when it comes to human cakes, there are additional options like chocolate, white, lemon, vegan… the list goes on and on. Even the article titled "Best" has over twenty variations.

"This would be so much easier if I could talk to the client in person," I grumble to myself. The *Romantasy's* crew members are only permitted to interact with cruise ship guests on an as-needed basis; I guess baking a special-order item isn't considered "needed."

I tap my fingers against the island countertop in time to the lyrics playing on my Integrated Communication Chip. I have the kitchen to myself, and only half the lights are on. The racks above the island counter in the center are empty, however, and maintenance tools cover one burnished metal countertop. This area is officially closed for renovations, but other than a hazard warning posted next to the garbage evacuation button, the appliances are fully functional. I brought my own utensils, and I'll have to clean up after myself, but the privacy is worth it.

Regardless of how unimportant the cruise director believes this special order to be, I'm going to give it my all. Not only does the client want to showcase this cake on a cooking show, I've learned that a judge for the Nebula Chef awards is on board, and I want to earn the first ever Nebula Star for Earth cuisine. Though I've never met someone from Earth, my matrix is currently in human form. I always assume the form of the species I'm cooking for; it helps me better understand their palate and culinary methods.

A recipe for something called a "Classic Bundt" pops up. Its shape reminds me of a Hypawan cuttlefish. I pause, considering. Should I go with classic or unique? If I choose something simple, I have to get the flavor and texture absolutely perfect. But the judge is likely to grant more leeway on something challenging. Pursing my lips, I continue scrolling.

I've spent the past few days cranking out mass orders for over four hundred passengers, and though I enjoy making people happy through food, I'm weary of making the same thing over and over. This cake will not only let me showcase my skills, it will bring joy to someone on a special day.

A recipe for cake doughnuts scrolls past, then something called a funnel cake. Both use a technique called "deep frying," which is basically boiling in oil. According to the servers I've spoken with, such items seem popular with the humans on the cruise, and the funnel cake looks like it will stack nicely between layers of frosting.

I shrug. Why not? If the results aren't satisfactory, I have time to start again.

Turning up my music, I start assembling the ingredients.

BETHANY

I grip the stem of a glass holding what passes for alien champagne in one hand while I pace near the service elevator on the *Romantasy's* observation deck. The strange spicy scents coming from the nearby hors d'oeuvres tables would usually intrigue me, but tonight I need to stay focused. My entire career could hinge on this slightly underhanded scheme, but it's not like I have a lot of options.

Overhead, the domed ceiling reveals a glowing yellow planet surrounded by multi-colored rings, while an alien orchestra plays a lively tune from a circular stage in the middle of the room. Nearby on the dance floor, I catch the familiar laugh of my oldest sister, Suzanne, as she waltzes by in the arms of a blue-skinned alien. At least she's having fun. I've lost track of my other two sisters, but I'm sure they're here too, as we're required to attend these nightly meat-markets as part of our free cruise package.

A winged alien with gray skin and horns sprouting from his forehead catches my eye and angles toward me, but I cross the edges of my pashmina over my chest and level my best resting bitch face in his direction until he changes course. I probably should've opted for something less sexy than my elegant black evening dress and stilettos, but there's a chance I'll need to shoot some selfies this evening, and I want to look my best.

I'm not on this cruise to have fun. My primary focus is the food—more specifically, the chefs. It's been two weeks since my producer threatened to cancel my baking show if I don't come up with a plan to improve ratings, and I was at a loss about what to do until my sister won tickets to this luxury space cruise. Aliens are all the rage since the galactic prince married a human last year, and hosting a real-life alien chef on my show could send ratings sky-high. My producer sure was salivating at the idea.

Yet here I am, three days in, and I have yet to even meet a chef in person. Apparently, the Intergalactic Dating Agency has a policy against staff mingling with guests, and no matter how much I protest, plead, or pout, the cruise director keeps denying my request. Everyone acts like I intend to jump the chef's bones on sight or something. The best I could do was commission one chef to bake my birthday cake as a demo.

I've bribed a steward to smuggle me into the kitchen so I can capture footage of the chef at work. I think the chef's Nebula Chef credentials will impress my producer, but the show is about more than just the food—the guests need camera appeal, and the only way to prove that is to capture footage of the chef in action. Once I have that, I can focus the rest of the demo on the show-stopping presentation and taste test. I can't afford to let this plan go sideways or I'll lose my show for sure. And I don't lose.

As I'm searching for my guide but trying not to be obvious about it, I notice a young woman with gorgeous black skin searching the buffet. Her eyes are red and glistening with tears, and her arms are crossed tightly over the front of her bronze cocktail dress.

"Are you all right?" I ask, checking behind her in case some creeper is trying to follow her.

Her breath hitches. "Do you know if there's any club soda around here?" She uncrosses her arms to reveal an ugly magenta stain on the neckline of her dress. "I need to get this out before it sets."

"No, I'm sorry." I grimace. "But club soda doesn't really work for stains, anyway."

She bites her lip, chin wobbling as if she's about to cry. "This is my only cocktail dress…"

I move closer to get a better look at the smudge. I can't tell what it is. "They probably have some sort of alien technology on board that can remove that for you by morning."

"Maybe. But I was hoping to clean up now." She smiles weakly. "It's not easy to flirt when you look like a slob."

Although I'm not here to meet alien men, most of the women on board are, and I feel bad for her. I remove my black silk pashmina and hold it out. "Here. See if this will cover it up."

She shakes her head. "I can't take your shawl!"

"It's fine, really. You need it more than I do." I drape it across her chest and let the long ends hang down her back like a dupatta. "See? Now nobody can see the stain."

She smiles with relief. "Thank you so much. How do I get it back to you?"

"I'm having a birthday party tomorrow in the restaurant on the lower deck." I've used a sizable portion of the show's marketing budget to book one of the ship's small restaurants for my birthday so I can showcase the alien chef's cake, and even invited the galactic crown prince, Arazhi, and his new human bride. Go big or go home, right? "Come to the party and you can return the shawl."

"Oh, wow! Happy birthday!" She hugs me. "I'll see you tomorrow. Thank you again." She heads back to the dance floor with a bright smile.

I watch her disappear into the crowd before once more searching the vast, crowded room. Where is my contact? I've been standing here since the party began. It's impossible for him to miss me.

Chewing my lip, I check the time on my phone for the tenth time in as many minutes. I paid in advance, so that little alien better not stand me up. Though if he does, I'm not certain I can tell one short gray alien from another enough to ream him out…

The elevator cycles open for what feels like the hundredth time tonight, and my pulse quickens. A thin gray alien wearing a white crew uniform steps into view. He looks like something straight out of the Roswell books, with an oversized head and huge dark eyes, and he hurries straight toward me. *Finally.*

"Are you ready, miss?" The alien glances nervously from side to side. "The corridor will be vacant for a brief span of time while the servers ready the next courses. We must be quick."

"Not a problem," I say and follow him to the circle on the floor. The lift descends with dizzying speed, making my already nervous stomach lurch. Maybe I should've avoided that drink. I'm still reeling as we come to a stop in the middle of a corridor intersection.

"This way." My escort hurries me down the passage. Unlike the ornately decorated guest areas of the ship, the walls and ceiling of this wide corridor are a featureless gray, though the deck is painted with symbols I can't decipher. If I didn't have the alien leading me, I'd be utterly lost down here. I pause to snap a photo of the symbol on the floor so I can get back on my own if I need to.

When I look up again, the alien is already several yards away. I run to catch up, my stilettos clicking against the hard deck. Ahead, the familiar bustle and clank of working kitchen staff echoes from an open hatch on the left. We slow as we approach, and my guide says, "We need to pass by here quickly." He peers around the corner, then beckons to me and whispers, "They're not looking. Hurry."

I tap the record button on my camera and aim it inside as I scurry past, barely daring to breathe. Three or four alien cooks move around stainless steel counters, too focused on their work to notice us. I'll take a better look at what I filmed them doing when this is all over. Maybe I can work some of it into the demo film.

We turn down another hall, moving past hovering carts of neatly folded linen before coming to a stop at a closed hatch. The small alien gestures toward it. "Chef Izhima is in here."

I hand him several of the credit chips we use onboard as tips, thinking it might be good to reinforce the bribe. "Thank you."

The alien grins, small mouth displaying what looks like glistening gray gums instead of teeth, and presses the door control. "Enjoy yourselves."

He scurries away as the door shushes quietly open. Music emerges from inside, a soprano voice singing in a language I can't understand.

Taking a steadying breath, I slip into a half-lit kitchen.

2

IZHIMA

I squeeze another artful loop of green frosting onto the stack of golden-brown funnel cakes when the sound of someone clearing their throat draws my attention.

Annoyed by the interruption, I glare over my shoulder. A human with auburn hair pulled away from her pale cheeks stands just behind me. She wears a black dress that hugs the curve of her waist and hips, slit to expose a considerable portion of her thigh. My heart cramps in my chest, and I suddenly understand why we're restricted from interacting with the humans; with her watching, I don't think I could concentrate enough to make a dumpling, much less cook for the entire cruise ship.

"You're not supposed to be in here, *tekina*," I say, using the galactic word for human. I can't afford to be distracted, but I also can't seem to take my eyes off her.

"I'll leave in a minute." Her pink lips spread in a winsome smile that makes my groin tighten. "I only need a few seconds of footage for the show."

My eyes narrow. The cruise director told me the human who ordered the cake is some sort of video celebrity on her planet. I glance at the order on my ICC to read the name I'm supposed to scrawl across the surface of the completed cake. They gave me the words in a dialect called English, and I sound out the phonetics as best I can. "Are you Beth?"

She ignores me, her gaze drifting to the stack of funnel cakes I've assembled. Her bright smile withers to a frown. My heart sinks. Though the confection isn't complete, I'm proud of how it's coming along. The whipped green frosting I concocted has a perfect balance of rich and sweet that won't overpower the delicate flavor of the cakes.

"Is that… my cake?" she asks. She's staring at it as if it's a delivery of three-day-old fish.

My *Iki'i* is overwhelmed by the itchy feeling of her dismay, yet I don't understand why. I set the piping bag aside and turn to face her fully. "Is this not what you expected?"

"Absolutely not. Where did you find the recipe for this… this… whatever this is?" Her annoyance feels like a flame thrower.

My own indignation rises. Perhaps I was wrong about why the crew is restricted from the human guests. This female is quite abrasive. I lift my chin. "I searched our database on human cake extensively to formulate this recipe. This will please the human desire for both fat and sugar."

"Oh, my God. You have no idea what you're doing." She strides past me and the island counter toward the appliances on the far wall as if she owns the kitchen.

"Now hold on—"

"We need to fix this. Fast." She glances around, veering toward the big door next to the garbage chute. "I need butter, eggs, sugar, flour—"

I hurry after her and grab her arm, my irritation barely in check. "This is my kitchen, and you're not supposed to be in here. Just tell me what's wrong, and I'll fix it."

She jerks away, her brown eyes flashing. "There's no way you can salvage this on your own. All of it's wrong. I'm not leaving this up to chance. Now where's your cooler?"

Before I can stop her, she reaches up and hits the button for the garbage chute.

"Wait, don't—" My words are sucked away as the door irises open and a hurricane of wind and flying utensils sweep through the kitchen. Normally, the chute opens to a repository that is ejected through a secondary airlock. An airlock which is apparently stuck open.

In less than a breath, we're swept out into black, empty space with the rest of the kitchen's contents.

I barely have time to assemble my wits, hardening my matrix to protect myself against the cold vacuum of space. But then I see Bethany spinning next to me, her face a mask of terror. The whites of her eyes are turning red, and crystals of frost are creeping across her skin.

Kuzara. She might be a pain in the ass, but if I don't do something, she'll be dead in mere moments. I stretch out a hand and pull her against me, encapsulating her in my matrix before hardening again. I've just cut my survival time down exponentially, but I've more than doubled hers. On my own, I can survive space quite a while in a state of hibernation, but maintaining oxygen and warmth for her will drain me quickly. I can only pray someone on board the *Romantasy* notices what happened before it's too late.

This damn female is going to be the death of us both.

I'm brought back to awareness by the return of gravity. Blessed air surrounds my matrix, and I release the female's body, collapsing into my amorphous resting state. I don't know how long we were floating out there or where we are now, but I'm too exhausted to do anything but lie here. *We survived.* I know because I could feel Beth's heartbeat in the moments before I released her.

My senses return slowly and in pieces. The deck I'm on feels grimy, and a low, persistent rumble tells me we're probably on an older ship with a plasma field drive. Voices are speaking around me, slowly becoming clearer to my muddled senses.

"What is that?"

The female's weight is lifted away. I ripple with relief. I hope this means a medic will arrive soon with a stim shot so I can get back on my feet. Better yet, a regeneration pod to bring me back to full health, though that's likely too much to hope for; most ships aren't equipped with Kirenai-specific medical units.

"Looks like a Vatosangan," a scratchy voice replies. At first, I think they're referring to me; my mother is Vatosangan. But I'm in my resting state, so they wouldn't know that. Then I realize they must be talking about the human. Few beings have seen the species in person, and I can see why they might mistake her for the alabaster-skinned Vatosangans.

"Ever see one with hair that color?" This voice draws out the vowels a little too long. "Feels like it's a female."

If I could frown, I would. What, exactly, are they feeling to determine she's female? I'm still too weak to use my *Iki'i* to sense the emotions in the room, but even without it, I'm getting an uncomfortable feeling about the situation.

"I think it's a human," says someone with a smooth Hypawan accent. "Do you know how much they go for on the black market?"

Kuzara. My instinct is right. Human females are highly sought after throughout the galaxy, as they are able to produce offspring with most other species. Nearly all the planets in the consortium have declining populations, and the desperate need for new genetics creates a thriving black market in breeding stock. This crew is obviously familiar with the trade.

I have a sinking feeling there won't be a stim shot coming my way. I need to come up with a plan. Drawing all my strength, I manage to look around.

Bethany lays sprawled on the deck an arm's length away, dress pulled halfway up her thighs. Her previously smooth, pale skin is mottled and red. An onyx-skinned Hypawan in gray coveralls squats beside her. Behind them, I see what looks like heaps of garbage and the gray outline of a closed metal hatch.

A scaled, pink Qalqan moves into view, bending down to grasp Bethany by the shoulders. "Let's get her to the med bay," he says in a scratchy voice.

Green hands with paddle-like fingers grasp her ankles, and I follow the arms up to see a Klen with a bent eyestalk. His skin is pocked by scars that indicate he survived the plague. "What about the Kirenai?"

The Hypawa shrugs, one long finger scratching his belly. "Jettison him if we're keeping the female. We'll ask the captain."

They disappear from my field of view, voices echoing down the corridor.

Adrenaline I didn't know I had spikes through my system. I have to pull myself together, not only for myself, but for the human. In agonizing increments, I begin solidifying into my human form. *Kuzara*, I'd much rather be baking a cake right now.

3

BETHANY

Something is very wrong.

Why is it so hot in here? Or is it cold? I can't tell the difference. All I know is pain.

I gasp for breath. The air stinks of engine oil, garbage and sweat. Opening my eyes is an impossible task, so I remain still, struggling to regain my senses. Male voices fade in and out around me. Loud. Indecipherable. My head pounds.

Slowly, I curl my fingers, muscles barely responding. *Where am I?*

I'm on my back, the surface beneath me hard as granite. Every inch of my skin hurts like I have a sunburn, right down to the soles of my feet. Even breathing burns my lungs like acid. What the hell happened to me?

I let out a groan and try to open swollen, gritty eyes. They feel glued shut. I put a hand up to my face and discover a cloth blindfold. I try to speak, but the words emerge as garbled slop that feels like molten lava clearing my throat.

"Whoa there, little human. Better leave that in place." A rough hand wraps around my knuckles and jerks my fingers from the blindfold.

Little human? Why would someone call me that? I have the gut-wrenching feeling I'm no longer on Earth. Panic wells up at the back of my throat and I lick my lips, trying hard to form words. What comes out is barely more than a scratchy whisper. "Where?"

"You're in what passes for a med bay on this space junker. We ain't got a fancy med-lab to drop you in, so you're going to have to recover the old-fashioned way. Lucky Naro spotted you out there when he did, or you'd be a space popsicle by now."

Space popsicle? Am I on a space ship? Somehow, that feels right. But I don't know why or how.

"What's your name, sweet thing?" His calloused thumb grazes along the backs of my knuckles. I don't like the false endearment or his tone, and even though I'm blindfolded, I swear I can feel his gaze on my breasts as I pull my hand free of his.

I open my mouth to answer him and panic spikes through me. *What is my name?* I realize I can't answer him. I claw at the fabric over my eyes again.

"I said no," calloused-hand guy says.

This time, both my hands are captured and restrained, my subduer's grip no longer pretending to be gentle. He shoves my arms down and plants what must be his elbow in my gut to keep me still. I scream and kick, trying to buck him off, but it's like trying to get out from under an anvil.

"Tie her up," a surprisingly mellow voice says. "She's worth less if she damages herself."

Worth less? To who? Terror growing, I thrash, forcing a single word from my parched throat. "What?" But the very act of breathing is an effort, and my attempts to speak are little more than gasps.

Bindings snake around my wrists, and I kick my feet as they secure more straps to my ankles. I'm forced to lie back, helpless, voiceless, and full of questions. Who are these men? How did I get here?

"Please," I croak out.

"Mmm, I like it when they beg." This third voice has an oily undercurrent that makes my blood turn icy. His voice draws closer. "You sure she belongs to him?"

"Don't know why else he'd protect her like that," says the first voice. "It was dangerous, even for a Kirenai."

I'm so confused, I simply lie there listening as my tears soak the blindfold.

"Pretty one like this has to be worth a lot. Maybe he was protecting his investment."

What feels like claws brush up the inside of my bare calf, catching on the hem of my skirt and sliding it up my thigh. "It's possible he won't recover. Especially if we help things along."

I cringe and squeeze my thighs together as best I can despite my bindings chafing my skin. This has to be a nightmare, right? I want desperately to wake up.

"Keep your hands off her girly bits, Pjo. At least until we know what she's worth."

The claws stop their advance but remain poised between my thighs. A sour waft of someone's breath hits the side of my face.

I twist my face away, drawing my shoulders up as if they can protect me.

"The black market's hot for humans right now," the oily voice speaks right next to my ear. "I wouldn't mind knowing what all the fuss is about."

The way these men—aliens?—talk about humans has me racking my insidiously empty brain for any scrap of information about how I got here. Why can't I remember? All I've pieced together is that I'm on what I think must be a space ship, I'm surrounded by aliens who think they should sell me on the black market, and I have no idea how I got here.

IZHIMA

Once I've fully assumed my human form, I can do nothing more than lie on the floor naked and panting. My nostrils flare at the rank scent of garbage and unwashed bodies. I know I need to get up, but my energy reserves are nearly depleted.

Then a female's scream echoes down the corridor. *Beth*.

I struggle to my feet. Though the human female got herself into this mess, she doesn't deserve whatever this crew has planned for her. Leaning against the bulkhead, I make my way down the corridor, gathering what strength I can for the coming confrontation. I need to appear strong and in charge if there's any hope of us surviving this crew.

Sounds of a struggle echo from an open hatch ahead. The female's screams have subsided to hoarse whimpers, and I hope I'm not too late. Just before I reach the opening, I hear the Klen's voice. "I say we airlock the Kirenai and take her for ourselves."

My fists ball, and I round the corner to see Bethany lying bound and blindfolded on top of a long cargo container surrounded by three crewmen. This bay looks more like a janitorial closet than a medical bay, with shelves holding both cleaning supplies and what look like bandages and antiseptics. A low cargo box scattered with medications sits against the wall just past the doorway.

The Klen has a green hand between the female's thighs, and the Qalqan grips the bindings around her wrists. The Hypawa's hands are in the pockets of his dirty gray coveralls, but I know he's less than innocent. Lascivious emotions fill the small bay and permeate my *Iki'i* like rancid oil infused with the sharp tang of Bethany's terror.

Standing tall, I step inside and stare straight at the Klen who suggested the airlock. "Back away from the human."

The Qalqan drops the bindings, his pink lizard-like face unreadable to my eyes and my *Iki'i* alike. His race is one of the few who are impervious to my senses. Qalqan also have innate medical intuition, and I'm sure he senses how exhausted I am. But he shuffles back a step. "Pjo was only joking. We'd never let him do that, of course."

Bethany rasps something unintelligible, but I think she's trying to ask for help.

The Klen's eyestalks twitch, and he crosses his green arms over his chest without moving. "Just having a bit of fun is all. No hard feelings."

"Yeah, if we were going to jettison you, we'd have already done it," adds the Hypawa.

But I can sense Pjo's scheming emotions. He really wants this female, and I have no doubt he'd kill me if given the chance.

I make a displeased "hmph" and pick up a water bottle from the nearby counter, chugging the contents. It's not a stim shot, but at least it's something, and I need fortification if I'm going to defend the female. Grabbing a second bottle, I move toward Bethany, keeping my head high and my shoulders back.

Fiery red splotches mottle her delicate skin, and her lips are chapped and flaking. I loosen her bindings, then help her sit and press the water to her lips. "Here, drink."

She takes several gasping gulps of water, then loops trembling arms around my neck. "Where are we?"

The once pushy, abrasive female is now quivering with fear. I find myself wanting to comfort her, despite my resentment that she's the entire reason we're here. *Kuzara*, what a pain in my ass. I should be back on the *Romantasy* preparing another fine meal for the Nebula Judge, not stuck on what appears to be a garbage scow acting as a bodyguard. Yet my drive to protect her seems to be ingrained within my very matrix.

"Let me handle this, Beth." I lift her against my chest and stare one by one at the crew, ending with a long hard look at Pjo. "Which one of you is going to take us to the captain?"

"No need." An unfamiliar voice startles me from the doorway.

I spin to find a G'nax filling the doorway, gray head spines flared in aggression.

4

BETHANY

"I'm the captain," says the unknown voice. It has a weird, clicky sound, and I think he must be alien, too.

But I'm already surrounded by aliens, so one more seems like no biggie, and right now I'm mulling over the name my rescuer called me. Beth feels right, yet also not right, like I'm missing the second half. But a surname can come later. For now, I'm just grateful to have an identity. *My name's Beth.*

"Have you notified the authorities of our rescue?" the man holding me demands, the deep rumble of his words resonating against my cheek.

I'm cradled against his very muscular, very *naked* chest. He feels human, and that small familiarity sends a shudder of relief through me. I don't know who this guy is, but at least it seems he wants to keep me safe.

"No authorities," the captain snaps.

Tugging my blindfold up off one eye, I strain to open my swollen lid. The light feels like a spear straight into my brain, and I hold my breath against the pain. Tears make everything blurry, but in the few seconds I can stand, I'm pretty sure the captain is gray and covered in spines. He looks like a cross between a bug and a human. Pointy protrusions that look like mandibles open and close as if he's agitated.

I squeeze my eye shut again, unable to bear the pain. Or the weirdness I just saw.

My rescuer is unfazed, however. His arms tighten around me, and his already rock-hard chest seems to expand. "Why no authorities?"

"This is a restricted area of space, and we don't exactly have permits."

"You're pirates." His voice is more challenge than question.

The captain makes another clicking noise. "Not exactly. This is a garbage scow."

"Scavengers, then," says the man holding me.

"We prefer to be called repurposing agents," one of the crew says, and the others chuckle. "Them cruise ships jettison a lot of valuable stuff."

"Like human females," Pjo croons in his greasy voice. "We could definitely repurpose her. Do you have proof she belongs to you, Kirenai? Because the laws of salvage make her ours unless you do."

A beat that feels thicker than tar passes. Then the baritone says, "I highly suggest you cease speaking of my mate as if she's property."

My heart skips a beat. *His mate?* I have no memory of a man in my life, let alone getting married. But how can I be certain when I don't even recall my own name? I rest my cheek against the corded muscle where his neck meets his shoulder, breathing in his unfamiliar but pleasant masculine scent that reminds me slightly of toasted almonds. His grip on my shoulders and legs is gentle, but still sends prickles of pain across my over-sensitized skin. What could've happened to me to make me like this?

Letting out a long breath, my supposed husband says, "Tell you what. Call the *Romantasy* to pick us up now, and I'll ask the captain to look the other way about your presence."

The *Romantasy*. The name feels familiar, a memory lingering at the edge of awareness. A cruise ship? Yes!

That's right. We're passengers—or were passengers. Maybe we were on our honeymoon? If we're newly married, it might explain why I can't remember my husband; short-term memory is the easiest to lose, right? And a cruise ship named *Romantasy* certainly sounds honeymoon worthy.

"Sorry, can't do that," replies the captain. "Couple of my men have records, and I can't risk getting my ship impounded. Best we can do is drop you at the next space station."

"For a fee, of course," a gruff voice adds. "You came off that fancy cruise ship, so you must be loaded."

"Listen," my husband says, and I can tell by his tone he's working hard to remain calm. "We don't have any money for ransom, if that's what you think. I'm not a guest. I'm one of the cruise chefs. My name is Izhima Amai."

Disappointment invades my chest. Not on our honeymoon then. But at least I know my husband's name now, and it feels right that he's a chef.

"What about her?" Pjo's insipid voice comes from close behind us. "And don't try to tell me she's one of the cleaning staff or something. Not in a dress like that."

Izhima's grip on me tightens painfully, and I once more force my eye open and quickly glance down my body. I'm dressed in a slinky black dress that exposes more skin than it covers—skin that's an angry, mottled red. What the hell caused that? I obviously need medical attention, yet these assholes can think of nothing but fucking me.

"What the hell is wrong with you people?" I rasp, anger firing my voice past my burning vocal cords. Through my teary vision, I see one alien has onyx skin and huge, liquid eyes that take up at least half his features. Another looks like a frog with extended eyestalks, and a third like a pink iguana. Froggy is leering at me, so I focus on him. "People will notice we're missing and come looking for us. If you call the authorities now, you'll be honored as heroes. If you don't, they'll still find us, but you'll be arrested as kidnappers."

"Whoa, she's a feisty one, isn't she?" says the onyx-skinned alien in a mellow voice, blinking in a way that reminds me of a sleepy lemur. It might have seemed adorable in other circumstances.

"You have no idea," my husband mutters.

"We missed a lucrative opportunity because we stopped to rescue you." The iguana's gruff voice has a frosty edge to it that makes me want to hide. "If you can't come up with adequate compensation, I'm sure you'll fetch a pretty penny on the black market, mated or not. Lot of species just want a taste."

"I'd call it square if she gave us a taste," says Pjo, licking his froggy lips.

I glare at him, but my eye is so watery and painful, I'm not sure he can interpret the look. "Touch me again and I'll serve your balls to you on a platter."

The crew laughs, but in a demeaning way.

Izhima leans close to my ear. "You're not helping. Do your sisters have any money?"

I have sisters? My head throbs trying to remember, but I can dredge up nothing. Feeling sick to my stomach, I crane my head to look at him and my breath hitches—this guy is handsome as fuck, with a defined jaw, generous lips, and dark eyes with no whites—but his skin is *blue*. Blue!

Did I marry an alien?

My head is spinning, and I'm forced to close my eyes again. I can't imagine marrying a non-human. Yet he says I'm his mate, and apparently risked his life to save me. Why would he do that if I didn't mean something to him? All I can do is shake my head no. No, no, no! This is all too much.

A soft exhale of his breath brushes my cheek, then he turns us back toward the captain. "We can earn our keep. I'll bet none of you have had a decent meal in a long time. I'm a Nebula Chef, one of the finest in the galaxy. We'd be happy to cook for you until we reach the next spaceport."

Behind us, the aliens start to murmur. I catch, "We could use a decent cook," and, "I've missed real food since Fherl jumped ship."

"Shut up, Naro," says Pjo. "We don't need a stupid cook, and what about the female? Everyone on board has to earn their bunk. That's the rule."

I grit my teeth, wanting to strangle him. But I'm also terrified. I need to offer legitimate value, or they'll demand payment between my legs. "I work with him in the kitchen, obviously," I say, not even sure if a Nebula Chef needs someone to help. For all I know, aliens have a technology to do that. "We're a team."

I feel Izhima nod. "Yes. She's my dishwasher."

I splutter. I may not know who I am, but I'm certain I'm not in charge of washing dishes. He squeezes me tighter, stalling my words.

"She prefers to be called a prep chef," he says in a conspiratorial tone.

The captain lets out several clicks, as if considering. At last he says, "We could do with some better slop than what Naro coaxes out of the defunct replicator. We'll vote on it after we've tasted our first meal. Until then, Choq, give them a bunk in the cargo bay."

The crew grumbles, but Izhima's already carrying me from the room. Eyes closed, I press my cheek against his warm chest. My adrenaline seems to have run out, and I'm clenching my teeth to keep from trembling violently. I focus on the facts I've gathered. My name is Beth. I was on a spaceship called the *Romantasy* and was in some sort of accident. I'm now trapped on a ship with a bunch of low-lifes who want to rape me. And, evidently, I'm married to an alien.

BETHANY

"You two sleep here," growls our escort as we come to a stop. "And don't even think about pocketing anything. It's all catalogued."

The air smells like a musty trash bin, and I breathe shallowly against Izhima's chest, grateful his toasted almond scent is delicious enough to somewhat mask the foul conditions.

I hear footsteps retreating, then Izhima sets me on my feet. "Can you stand on your own?"

"I think so." But I totter, unable to balance on my stilettos.

He catches my arm before I fall. "Sit."

Guiding me back onto what feels like a metal crate, he lowers me onto it. The surface is sticky under my fingertips, and I surge unsteadily upright once more. "Ugh! What's been spilled here?"

I yank the blindfold off my head. Tears spill over my cheeks in burning rivulets, and my nose is running, but at least the lights here aren't blinding. I use the blindfold to wipe my nose and look down. The crate is one of many in a maze of unrecognizable junk surrounding us. Nearby, I spot a single, narrow cot nestled between the foul-smelling stacks. "Do they actually expect us to sleep here?"

"Yes, and be grateful for it." Izhima says between gritted teeth. For the first time since waking, I get a good look at the man I'm supposed to be married to. He's absolutely stunning—tall and broad-shouldered, with smooth cobalt skin and nearly black hair and eyebrows. To my shock, he's completely naked. My eyes widen at the sight of the generous cock hanging between his legs. I muffle a surprised cough and press my legs together against the sudden rush of wet heat. *Why don't I remember that?*

"Where are your clothes?" I gasp.

As if my words are a physical touch, his shaft swells and lifts. "I had to shed them when I saved you."

I gulp, forcing my gaze back up to his face. His eyes are a solid dark blue that's nearly black with no white. He seems completely unabashed by his state of undress. And why should he be? He's gorgeous. "You saved me? From what?"

"You don't remember?"

I grimace and shake my head. "I think I have amnesia."

He rubs a wide blue hand over his mouth. "*Kuzara.* How bad?"

"How the hell should I know?" I scowl, all my fear and frustration rising like soda in a bottle that's been shaken. "I didn't remember my own name until you said it. Why would you ask a person with amnesia how bad they have it?"

His lips thin as he stares at me. A fleeting memory wisps across the edge of my consciousness. I think I've seen that angry stare before. I lift my chin and face him squarely. Even without remembering my past, I know I'm not one to back down from a fight.

But instead of laying into me, he lets out a loud breath. "Stay here."

He stalks off between the rows of junk and disappears through a hatch.

My anger deflates, and my legs tremble so badly I'm forced to sit on the crate, sticky or not. I shouldn't have snapped at him. "Sorry. I guess I'm a bitch when I'm agitated," I mutter. But he's already gone.

IZHIMA

I stalk toward the med bay, throttling my anger at the frustrating female. I get that she's exhausted—we both are—but just because she's frightened and confused doesn't mean she has the right to treat me like I'm the bad guy. She's the one who vented us out of the airlock, not me. I'm the one who should be furious because instead of impressing the Nebula Judge on board the *Romantasy*, I'm stuck cooking slop for a bunch of garbage pirates.

Kuzara, I need a stim right now.

The corridor appears empty, but I keep my *Iki'i* wide open. I don't trust the crew, especially the Klen, Pjo. He's looking for an opportunity to take what he wants —and what he wants is the female. Leaving her alone right now is probably not a good idea, but she's in no condition to be walking and I'm in no condition to keep carrying her. I have to get my strength up so I can get us both through this unscathed.

Rounding the corner, I'm relieved to find the med bay empty. I rifle through the medications on the shelves.

It's probably a good thing the crew didn't offer assistance while I was in my resting state—everything seems to be expired or damaged. I locate a half-empty stim vial and shoot a dose into my thigh. A surge of warm energy floods my matrix, and I let out a relieved sigh..

My attention falls on a packet of painkillers. I'm fairly certain the crew didn't bother to think of Beth's comfort any more than they did mine. Perhaps her mood will improve if she's not in pain. If only I had a pill to cure amnesia. Though I'm not sure getting her memory back would improve her disposition.

I groan inwardly when I remember that she not only can't recall her own name; she believes we're mates. Our lives depend on her pretending to love me, but based on our brief interaction back in the *Romantasy's* kitchen, I doubt she even likes me. Will she be able to keep up the ruse if she has her memory back? I don't know if she's capable of controlling her reckless behavior or her impulsive tongue.

Perhaps it's better if she remains oblivious. One wrong word and she'll be sold on the black market while I get shoved out an airlock—again. And I'm not letting that happen.

I pick up the painkillers and head back to our bunk, resolved to keep the secret for her own good. Both of our lives depend on this lie. I just hope her amnesia lasts as long as our journey.

BETHANY

I hear something move among the stack of junk and stiffen, afraid it might be one of the crew coming for me. Then I spot a wiry tail disappearing beneath a crate and realize it's only a rat. *Or whatever passes for rats on an alien ship.*

I shudder and draw my arms around myself. My skin looks awful, but at least my dress isn't damaged, for what that's worth. I doubt I can get a change of clothing around here. I run my fingers over the silky fabric covering my thigh, wondering why I'm wearing something so fancy. It looks like something for an elegant party, not a crew uniform. *Maybe we really are wealthy guests.* Could Izhima have been lying about being a chef?

Yet he'd sounded so certain, and these aliens expect us to cook five-star cuisine. *Nebula* star cuisine. I'm not even certain what that is, but it sounds exotic. Although I'm pretty sure I know my way around a kitchen, who knows what these aliens consider food? Then again, judging by the smell of this cargo bay, I doubt this crew will be very discerning.

Izhima reappears with a bucket in one hand and a flask in the other. He sets the bucket on the floor, then hands me a pill and the flask. "This will help with the pain."

I gratefully swallow the pill with several gulps of tepid water. My eyes are on fire, and my skin doesn't feel much better. I want to sleep, but my mind is too full of questions.

Izhima looks tired, and I vaguely remember one of the crew saying something about what he did to save me being dangerous. I hand the flask back. "So what exactly landed us in this shitty predicament?"

He takes a drink. "We had an argument. You pushed the button controlling the airlock."

"I did what?" I gape at him, my mind a complete blank.

"You vented us."

"I can't believe I'd do something like that." I shake my head. I have amnesia, but I know I don't have a death wish. "What were we fighting about?"

"Your birthday cake."

I frown, even more doubtful. "I almost killed us over a birthday cake?"

His face softens. "In all fairness, you didn't mean to vent us. You were looking for ingredients. I'm fairly sure you thought you were opening a cooler."

While still difficult to believe, an accident seems much more plausible, especially on an alien ship. "So we were floating in space without a ship when they picked us up?" No wonder I have amnesia. I was without oxygen for who knows how long. It's lucky we're not dead. "How did you save me?"

"I engulfed you." He extends the hand holding the flask. Like liquid, his hand and forearm seem to dissolve, encasing the flask until his arm looks like a weird mallet with a flask shaped head.

I suddenly feel dizzy and have to brace myself upright on a trembling arm. "Holy shit. What kind of alien are you?"

"I'm Kirenai." Izhima's face twitches, and without warning, he picks me up and deposits me onto the cot. "Lay down before you fall over."

Though the mattress looks primitive, it seems to be made of some sort of advanced tech that's softer than I expect. Still, it will be close quarters for both of us to sleep on. I stare up at him, trying to focus only on his face and not the enormous penis dominating my field of vision. Despite my wooziness, I'm struck by the urge to touch it.

I shift my gaze away and stammer, "Do you think... would one of the crew loan you a set of clothes?"

A frustrated look fleets across his features. Pivoting, he yanks something from beneath my feet and wraps it around his waist. Now covered in a thin blanket, he asks, "Better, princess?"

I get the feeling he doesn't call me princess out of affection. *We were fighting before all this happened, and I did almost kill us.* I lick my lips, wondering if makeup sex would be out of the question right now. My skin hurts, but the painkiller he gave me seems to be kicking in already. I reach up and take his hand. "I'm sorry I vented us. Cake is the most important meal of the day, but it's not worth dying over."

His brows rise. "Ah. I did not know it was supposed to be a full meal."

I laugh. "That was a joke."

Izhima is less than amused, however, and pulls his hand from my grasp. Turning away, he draws a rag from the water bucket, ringing it out. "I see."

I clear my throat, suddenly feeling awkward. How can I feel so strained around the man I'm supposed to love? Hoping to jog my memory about how to interact with him, I ask, "How did we meet?"

"In the kitchen, of course." He wipes down the top of the sticky crate. His bare back flexes as he scrubs. I wonder if we ever cooked together while naked. A small fantasy rolls through my mind of licking frosting off his skin, but I have a feeling that didn't happen, not if we were fighting about cake in the first place.

I really wish I could scratch up at least one of my memories. Perhaps sleep would help. And I wouldn't mind snuggling in Izhima's arms. "You must be as exhausted as I am. Come lay down."

He stops scrubbing but doesn't turn around.

"Come on." I try to scoot over to the edge of the small cot. "I'm too tired to bite right now, even if you want me to."

Turning to look over his shoulder, he regards me with those dark eyes. "That is another joke?"

I laugh again. "Correct. Now get over here. We're going to have to cook soon, and we both need some rest."

He regards me another moment, then turns back to his scrubbing. "We can't both rest at the same time. One of us needs to keep watch."

Shit. He's probably right. I sit up and plant my feet on the floor. "Then you sleep first. You're the Nebula Chef earning our keep here, so you have to be well rested."

He dips the rag into the bucket again and starts washing the floor around the crate. I have to admit I'm impressed. A man who knows how to clean is sexy. But he's also stubborn. He speaks without turning around.

"You can't even stand up, and I'm going to need you in the kitchen. Sleep. I'll rest later."

Much as I want to argue, he's right. My eyes hurt too much to stay open any longer. I sink back onto the cot and let my lids drift closed, listening to him scrub until sleep takes me.

6

BETHANY

I blink awake, hoping everything was just a dream. But the dingy ceiling panels overhead are just as I remember, and I'm covered in a rough blanket that prickles my sensitive skin. I raise one arm to examine it. Though the skin feels tight, I think it looks a little less red, and I'm in nowhere near as much pain as I was before I fell asleep. I roll onto my side and see that an area around the cot is now clean. The air also smells slightly less pungent.

Izhima is sitting on the floor with his back against a crate, head bowed. His torso and legs now look like they're clothed in coveralls the same color as his azure skin. His broad shoulders and muscular thighs fill out the uniform perfectly, and now that I have a chance to

45

really examine him, I have to admit he's very good looking. He sits so still, I think he must be asleep, but then he looks up and meets my gaze.

Heat floods my cheeks as I realize he caught me staring at him. "How long did I sleep?" I stammer.

He stands slowly, moving as if his muscles don't want to obey. "A while."

From deeper in the bay, someone shouts. "She awake yet? I can't keep working on an empty stomach."

Izhima tilts his head toward the voice. "The crew has been asking for their meal."

I sit up so quickly, my head spins. "Why didn't you wake me? You haven't had a chance to rest."

"I'll be fine."

I squint toward his chest. Something looks off about the fabric, as if holes are forming and disappearing before my very eyes. I point uncertainly toward the area. "Is that… normal?"

He looks down and quickly smooths his hands across the area. The coveralls seem to shimmer, melt, and reform solidly over his skin. "I rarely have to do this."

I blink, realizing he didn't find clothes—he just made his skin look like coveralls the same way he wrapped his hand around the water bottle. I'm torn between being repulsed and thinking that has to be the coolest ability ever.

Pushing aside the blanket, I stand, the deck chilly against my bare feet. He must've covered me with the blanket he was wearing. Every time I turn around, he's taking care of me. *We really must be married.*

I spot my stilettos neatly placed beneath the cot and bend down to retrieve them. Working in a kitchen in heels won't be fun. Then I remember Izhima said I'm a freaking dishwasher.

Frowning, I look back up at him. "I'm not really a dishwasher, right?"

Though his features barely change, I swear he smirks at me. "Recently promoted to prep chef, remember?"

I narrow my eyes. "Hey! Girl with amnesia here. I can't tell when you're joking."

His eyes tighten a fraction. "I never joke." Turning away, he strides down a cleared path between the row of junk. "Come."

I stand there a moment. Never joke? Is he serious? I would never marry a guy without a sense of humor. Would I? Then I realize he's probably acting like this because he's holding a grudge about the fight I don't remember. Perhaps he's justified—I did nearly kill us, after all. Still, I can't help feeling a little salty about how stingy he's being with information.

With a sigh, I scurry after him. The way his blue coveralls hug his ass as he walks is distractingly sexy. *Not coveralls, that's actually his ass.* I lick my lips. So weird, but still sexy. I bet makeup sex is going to be off the charts—whenever that might be. After the cold shoulder he gave me last night, I'm going to have to charm those pants right off him.

Catching up, I loop my arm through his. "Any chance a prep chef can sleep her way to the top around here?"

He stiffens and gives me a surprised look. I think he's going to shrug me off, but just then the onyx-skinned crewman rounds the corner, and Izhima clamps my arm against his side.

The crewman is wearing a grease-smudged jumpsuit the same color as the walls. Unfamiliar tools dangle from his belt. He eyes Izhima's new clothes before letting his gaze fall to my cleavage. Damn this stupid sexy dress. I wish I had a shawl or something to cover myself.

"I'm Naro," he says. "Ship's engineer. Captain told me to show you to the galley."

"All right," says Izhima, still holding tight to my arm. I love how solid and warm his ribs feel beneath my touch, and step closer.

Izhima's stance remains rigid, and he keeps his gaze on Naro, even though the alien has now turned to walk down a corridor with pipes running along the walls and ceiling. I tilt my head to look up at Izhima's profile, but he doesn't even spare me a glance, just pulls me alongside him as he follows the engineer.

"I'm sure glad you're going to take over," Naro says as we pass a couple of closed hatches. His hair hangs in a thick black braid down his back, ending in what looks like a spiked metal bead as big as my fist. I also note that his fingers seem to have an extra joint, making them long and thin and very alien. "I'm tired of taking flak about the food. It's lucky I got the replicator working at all after the tantrum Fherl threw before he jumped ship, but it only spits out a few basics." He stops at an archway where the pipes make a sharp turn into another room.

We pause behind him, and I see we've reached a medium-sized kitchen with a crusty rectangular dining table bolted to the floor in the center that looks like it could seat ten or twelve. Two benches flank the table, and what looks like a year's worth of spills and crumbs splotch the floor. Something that resembles a cockroach scuttles from underneath the table and disappears beneath a bank of cupboards.

I plaster myself tightly against Izhima's side. Even with amnesia, I'm fairly certain I've never seen a kitchen this disgusting.

"We have a few staples in the cupboards. You'll have to use the replicator for anything else." Naro points a crooked finger toward what looks like two grimy windows set into the back wall with knobs and dials below them. One of the panes is damaged, jagged shards of glass clinging to the frame.

"You actually prepare food in here?" I ask.

Naro grins. "Not anymore. That's your job now, sweet thing."

My hackles rise at the condescending endearment, but before I can respond, Izhima says, "Don't call her that."

"What am I supposed to call her, then? You never told us your mate's name."

"I'm standing right here, asshole," I say, standing taller and glad for the added height of my stilettos. I hate it when men try to dismiss me. "And my name is Beth."

Naro doesn't break his gaze from Izhima's. But after a heartbeat, he nods. "Okay, Beth."

With a grimace, Izhima releases my arm and steps into the kitchen. He opens a panel that drops into a countertop with storage space behind it. "How many are we cooking for, Naro?"

"Only four of us here with Fherl gone."

Izhima nods and continues digging through the cupboard.

I remain in the archway, skin crawling at the thought of how many food-borne illnesses are probably lurking in this room.

"Why do you have so much *kazhitu* paste?" Izhima asks, holding out two green rectangular packets with yellow writing on them.

"We salvaged it off one of the cruise ships," Naro answers. "Don't use the ones that smell bad."

My stomach flip-flops. Did they salvage whatever *kazhitu* is from the trash? And now expect us to cook with it? I hug my arms over my stomach. "How long before we reach a spaceport?"

Naro's enormous eyes tighten to slits, making him look like an angry black lemur. "You haven't earned your passage yet, female."

Though it wasn't a direct threat, I take a step back. "I was just asking."

"We'll get there when we get there." Naro taps one of the many pipes lining the walls. "If the replicator acts up, try banging on this duct. I have to get back to the engine room." He brushes past me into the hall, pausing only long enough to say, "Captain wants to eat at eighteen hundred. I suggest you be ready."

7

IZHIMA

Now that Naro is gone, I sort through the packages in the cupboard while Beth stands in the doorway, hesitating with disgust. Some of the food packages are unmarked, while others are expired or too damaged to consume, but I find a few that are usable. Now I just need to come up with a meal the crew will enjoy eating.

Beth moves forward to peer over my shoulder. "What should I do?"

The last thing I need is more of her interference. Without looking her way, I say, "Clean this place up and make sure we have clean dishes."

I can sense her disappointment, but after a pause she says, "Okay. I'll go get the bucket from our bunk area."

"No," I turn to stop her. "You mustn't go anywhere on this ship alone. Look for what you need in the cupboards."

She grimaces and nods. Using the tip of a finger, she opens a tall cupboard, releasing a cascade of bottles and packages. She dances backward as items pile around her feet, nearly losing her balance on her high heels.

"Why are they keeping this trash?" She picks up what appears to be an empty wrapper.

I shrug. I don't have the energy to speculate. All my focus needs to be on the meal. "No idea, but they must have a reason. Try to stuff it back in there."

She bends over and reaches for something at the bottom of the cupboard. A flash of white darts up her bare arm. Her scream is like a spear in my chest, sending my heart into overdrive. She stumbles backward, half falling against the table.

Most vermin aren't actually harmful, but a *nezumi* bite can get infected if not treated properly. I rush to her side, spinning her to face me. "Are you all right?"

"There was something living in there!" She tilts her chin toward the pile of rags.

I run my palms along her arms, examining her pale skin. "Likely a *nezumi*. Did it bite you?"

"I don't think so." But she's trembling, and her fear is sour against my *Iki'i*.

"Let me see." Her skin has regained a healthier color, and when I run my fingers over the curve of her shoulder, I can't help enjoying the smooth, warm feel. I lift her hair to check the side of her neck, aware of a tightness developing in my groin. *What the hell am I doing?* Jaw tight, I drop my hands and force a step back. "You're fine."

Biting her bottom lip, she crosses her arms over her chest. "Thank you."

My resolve melts. Apparently, her vulnerability is addictive, too. "You're welcome." I grab a handful of rags, shaking them out to be certain they're clear of vermin before I hand them to her. "All clear."

She gingerly accepts the filthy tatters of cloth. "Don't suppose they have a washing machine around here?"

I show her the button to open the sink basin. "Best I can do."

While she washes the rags, I stuff the fallen garbage back into the cupboard. I don't know what it is about this *tekina* that inspires this strong urge to protect her, but I can't seem to stop myself from seeing to her wellbeing, even when her assailant is nothing more than a harmless *nezumi*.

Using a shoulder to force the cupboard door closed, I wink at her. "I don't recommend opening that again."

"Thank you." She rewards me with a smile and starts scrubbing off the galley table with the now clean rags.

Her smile pleases me more than it should. I turn away, adjusting the replicator's antiquated dials to create the vegetables I need for the meal. Sparks fizzle behind the broken glass and I swear. If I can't get the replicator to make even basic vegetables, we're going to be in real trouble.

"Do we use a replicator in our kitchen?" Beth asks.

Her reference to *our* kitchen makes me uncomfortable, but the replicator dials are taking up all my attention at the moment. "Yes, but I think this unit's older than my grandfather."

"Oh." She scrubs for a few more minutes while I wait for the replicator to produce a green-skinned *menchisu* and some protein-rich slabs of *butani*. I'm in the middle of peeling when she asks, "Have we been married very long?"

I should've known the questions would come. And here in the galley is definitely not the place or time for me to come clean. There's no telling who might be listening, either on surveillance or just around the corner in the corridor. I keep my eyes on the long curl of green skin I'm carving off the *menchisu*. "We haven't known each other long, no."

A small crease forms between her eyebrows. "What was my maiden name?"

I glance toward the open door to the galley. "I'm sure it will all come back to you. Just give it time."

"Why are you being so dodgy?" She dumps her bucket of dirty water and turns to frown at me. "It's a simple question."

"I'm not being dodgy." I say, meeting her eyes. "But I think it would be better if you remember on your own."

"You've got to be kidding me." She plants her hands on her hips. "You can at least tell me my name."

I sigh. Dredging up a name I recall reading while perusing recipes for her cake, I say, "Fine. Crocker… Beth Crocker."

She closes her eyes, mouth pursed as if tasting the name. "It doesn't feel right."

"See what I mean?" Hoping to stave off further questions, I ask, "Are you finished cleaning yet? I need to get on the prep work if I'm going to have a meal ready in time."

She glances at the filthy table and sighs. "No."

While she returns to scrubbing, I cut the *butani* and work on seasoning the crust. I sample everything as I work, not only as a chef, but because the nutrition helps me regain my energy levels. It will take a long time for me to regain full health this way, but I'm already feeling much better.

I'm pureeing some sauce when Beth suddenly stops working and stares at her fingertips. "Why are my nails polished?"

Her alarm is palpable to my *Iki'i*, but I stay calm, unsure where this might be going. Glancing at her crimson fingernails, I shrug. "I can't answer that. I suppose it's a human style."

"But chefs don't wear nail polish," she says, her voice louder than I'd like. "It's against code. Why are mine painted?"

I turn around to stir the soup. Her distress is creating an alarming pressure against my *Iki'i*, but I'm not sure how to answer her. Then I remember Pjo's comment about her fancy dress. "The same reason you're dressed in that expensive gown."

"Okay. And why am I wearing this?"

I dredge up everything I can remember about what the steward who gave me the order for the cake told me about her. "You were, um, I believe you called it interviewing? On the *Romantasy*."

"Interviewing?" She comes over to stand beside me, a crease between her eyebrows. "Why?"

"For a cooking show."

The suspicion crowding against my *Iki'i* lightens, and she grins. "Now I remember. I'm the star of a cooking show."

Her annoying ego has returned. I know I should just let it go, but I can't help myself. I shrug and say, "Well, technically, the chef is the star."

The joy in her eyes fades. "So, you're the star?"

Great. Now I feel bad. "I'm teasing you."

"My crew is going to mutiny if we don't eat soon." A voice from the hallway startles me, and I spin to see the captain standing in the entry, mandibles twitching.

I gesture toward the chopped orange vegetable with my knife. "The prep work is almost finished. I'll have a first course ready soon."

The captain opens and closes three-pincered hands. "What are you preparing?"

"*Ekitai* consommé and smoked *menchisu*. Followed by a *chomma* and *tomen* crusted *butani* with a side of poached *xeru*."

I sense awe and appreciation from both the captain and Beth.

"All right, then. You have an *irn*." The captain looks pointedly in Beth's direction. "Otherwise, the crew will look for something else to satisfy their appetites."

8

BETHANY

After the captain departs, Izhima peels, chops, stirs, and sautés while I clean the rest of the kitchen. I scrub hard and fast, too focused to ask any more questions. Plus, I don't want to distract him. My virtue relies on what I hope are his very skilled hands.

What feels like several hours later, I'm on my hands and knees scrubbing the floor when the crew arrives. They tromp in, snuffling like a herd of pigs in search of truffles.

"Smells decent," says the captain, dropping to a seat on the nearest bench.

"Never saw the place so shiny," says the pink lizard alien, also taking a seat, his stumpy tail hanging down over the bench.

Pjo sidles toward me, eyestalks undulating as he stares down my cleavage. "It does look pretty good."

I scramble back onto my feet, hands clenching the rag. Good thing I'm not holding a prep knife, because I'd probably stab his bulging, froggy throat at the moment.

Izhima steps between us and sets a tureen in the middle of the table. What looks like orange flower petals are scattered over a grayish broth. "Our first course is *ekitai* consommé." He passes out empty bowls and sinks a ladle into the tureen, setting the petals swirling. "After that, you'll enjoy a course of crusted *butani* and poached *xeru*."

The captain pats the bench beside him. "You sit here, female."

"That's all right. I'm not hungry." I shake my head and offer my most winning smile.

The captain makes a clicking noise with his mandibles. "Sit."

Pjo slides over on the bench, mouth in a too-wide smile. "There's room on this side, if you prefer."

"I've been cleaning all day," I say, putting my hands on my hips. "I'm filthy."

"Sit down so we can eat," says Naro. The extra joints on his fingers make it look like there are spider legs wrapped around his empty bowl.

I give Izhima a beseeching glance, but he nods. Gritting my teeth, I wash my hands while Izhima fills bowls, then I sit on the edge of the bench next to the captain. There's a bowl waiting for me, too, but I'll be damned if I eat anything made in this cesspool.

Naro pulls his bowl closer, taking a deep breath from the rising steam. "Mmmmm."

"Wait." The pink lizard points to the bowl in front of me. "You taste first."

"Me?" I gawk in horror at the gray broth. "Why me?"

"How else are we going to know you ain't trying to poison us?" asks Pjo.

I cross my arms. "Why would we poison you? Then we'd have no one to fly this ship. Besides, if you get sick, it's not our fault. Everything in your cupboards looks like it came out of the garbage."

"People throw away perfectly good food all the time," says Naro. "Now hurry up. I'm hungry."

Now that I'm not immersed in cleaning products, I have to admit the steam coming from the bowl smells savory and good. The gray soup looks strange, but I don't think Izhima would allow me to eat something that would kill me. And I watched him taste test things the entire time he cooked. I sigh and reach for the bowl. There are no spoons, so I lift it and take a small sip. The broth warms my tongue and spills down my throat. It has a buttery, slightly sweet flavor with a hint of citrus. Before I know what I'm doing, I take a second gulp.

The crew bursts into motion, lifting their bowls and slurping loudly.

I meet Izhima's eyes across the table. He's standing near the counter and watching me with rapt attention. I swallow again, and his gaze drops to my throat, then lower to the tops of my breasts above the neckline of my dress. My body warms from more than the delicious soup.

As if suddenly recognizing this is not the time or place to exchange sultry gazes, he turns his attention to removing the empty tureen from the table.

"Delicious, but not very filling," complains the lizard man, staring at my half-full bowl.

I curl my lips. Like I'm going to share with that asshole. I pointedly finish the rest. The orange flower petal things have a smoky, cheese-like flavor and texture. Overall, an exquisite first course, I must admit, even if the presentation was lacking. It needed a garnish, and a true consommé should've arrived already dished out, not served family-style. *Now, where did that thought come from?* Perhaps I really am the host of a cooking show.

Izhima sets a platter of what looks like slabs of tofu covered in black sesame seeds in the center of the table. The slabs rest on a bed of what looks like white marbles. "Crusted *butani* and poached *xeru*," he announces.

The crew members reach for the food excitedly, using their hands rather than the flat serving spoon Izhima provided. The pink lizard picks up his entire square of what I assume is *butani* in one hand and lifts it to his mouth.

"Hold up, Choq," says Naro, putting a long-fingered hand on the lizard's wrist. "Just because the soup isn't poisoned doesn't mean everything is safe." He looks meaningfully my way.

The rest of the crew now turns expectantly toward me.

I roll my eyes. This is ridiculous. Yet after tasting the soup, I have to admit I'm curious about the other courses.

Izhima is once more looking at me intently. "Go on, *tekina*," he says.

My breath catches as a flash of memory washes through me—Izhima's blue tongue and lips calling me *tekina. Is that his pet name for me?* I smile at him, hoping he's on his way to forgiving me, and reach for the serving spoon.

A mere scattering of white spheres and a broken chunk of the *butani* remains, which I hope broke during cooking and not because one of these louts manhandled it with their filthy claws before putting it back. I scrape together a few of the spheres plus half of the broken *butani* and put it on my plate. The dish smells a bit like bacon. My mouth waters. I adore bacon.

The single eating utensil next to my plate reminds me of a two-tined spork with a serrated edge. I cut into the crusty outside of the *butani* with ease and place a small morsel on my tongue. The crust is light and crunchy, but the interior almost melts on my tongue. It not only smells like bacon, it tastes like it, too.

I beam at Izhima. "Amazing as always, chef."

He looks momentarily flustered, a dark flush creeping over his azure cheeks. Then he turns away, busying himself with the next dish. I take a beat to appreciate his bare broad shoulders, then remind myself that he's tired and wants this over with so he can rest.

I sample the white spheres, shocked to discover they have a kick of spice, a heat that comes and goes quickly, leaving behind a salty sweetness I find delightful. The pairing of these flavors is amazing, and before I know it, my plate is clean. I reach for the platter and the other half of my serving, but Choq has already shoveled it onto his plate and is happily munching away, his lizard lips smacking loudly. *Asshole.*

The captain wipes his mandibles on a napkin with surprising daintiness and stands. "That was a fine meal. I'll expect an equally fine breakfast tomorrow."

"Isn't there more?" asks Pjo. "What about dessert?"

Everyone else had been getting to their feet, perfectly content, but now they look at Izhima expectantly.

A spike of fear rises in my chest. There's no doubt in my mind about where Pjo wants to take this thread. I stiffen, ready to bolt if things go south.

Izhima puts one hand on my shoulder, keeping me planted on the bench, and speaks to the captain. "Regretfully, we didn't have time to plan a dessert, not with the limited supplies at hand. We'll surpass your expectations tomorrow."

That seems to satisfy the captain, who nods. "See that you do."

"It was a tasty meal," mutters Choq on his way out. "Thank you."

Naro follows him. "I feel all fancy. Wonder what we get to eat next time?"

Pjo's eyestalks undulate, sliding from Izhima to me to the captain. Then he stands and heads toward the exit as well. "There'd better be dessert tomorrow."

My heart is still racing like a mixer on high speed, however, because the captain is now looking directly at me. "Still not sure the crew thinks this was enough for both your passages," he says, looking around the galley. "Though I do like how you've tidied the place. I suppose if you continue with the rest of the ship, we'll call it even."

I recoil. "The rest of the ship? You have to be kidding."

"Everyone has to earn their bunk."

"But Izhima needs me. I'm his prep chef." Not that I did any actual food prep, but the captain doesn't know that.

He shrugs. "We're a small operation. We all have multiple duties. Consider cleaning one of yours."

I glance at Izhima, hoping for some backup, but he's already putting items back into the cupboards. Resisting the urge to groan, I grab a rag and start washing the table for the second time today. These garbage collectors better get me to a spaceport soon, or they just may find themselves poisoned after all.

9

IZHIMA

I organize the ingredients for tomorrow's breakfast while Beth finishes cleaning. My gaze keeps sliding toward her when she isn't looking. Her compliments about my food surprised me, but not nearly as much as my own reaction to watching her eat. From the way her hands cradled the soup bowl to the wet pink tip of her tongue when she licked her lips, I found myself mesmerized. A strange stirring has risen inside me, a desire I don't want to acknowledge. But even as I try to push the thoughts away, they keep creeping back in. Unwelcome and undeniable.

Her back is to me as she dries the dishes, her shoulders bare in her fancy dress. She's quick and efficient, her delicate hands making quick work of the job. My heart thuds harder when I think about those hands touching me. I can't help but imagine lifting her auburn hair away from her neck and kissing her there. Breathing in her scent. Letting my hands roam where they will.

It can't be. If she's my mate, I should've sensed something the moment we met. Except the moment we met, I was so busy defending my cooking, I couldn't see anything else. Now that we've spent time together, I want to know everything about her. Where she grew up, what her family is like, what she loves besides cooking. I want to give her all the little things that make her happy.

Except she doesn't remember these things herself.

She turns around and gives me a weary smile. "I'm done. Anything you need help with?"

Kuzara, now she's being considerate, too? It has to be the amnesia. Once she gets her memory back, I'm sure I'll find her as frustrating as ever. The Beth I first met is still in there somewhere. I saw it when she argued with the crew about sitting down to eat and again when she argued with the captain about cleaning the ship. Much as I might be tempted to tell her the truth, I can't risk it.

"I'm ready to go," I say and gesture toward the door.

She loops one arm through mine and pulls me along beside her. The contact with her skin sends a thrill through my matrix, and I'm glad we're both tired, or I might do something I regret. After a quick stop at the lavatory, we head to our bunk, and she immediately slumps onto the cot.

"Come lie down." She pats the mattress next to her, her smile tired.

The temptation is great—both to lie down and to be near her. I sit on a nearby crate instead. "You rest. I still don't trust the crew."

She scowls and stretches a hand toward me. "Stop arguing and get over here. If we're together, they can't snatch me out of your arms without you knowing. Besides, I'm cold."

I pause and consider. Could she be right? If I'm with her, I can protect her better. But the mattress is narrow, and we would have to lie almost on top of one another. Much as I desire that—and more—I also need rest, and I would get no sleep that way. Sighing, I stand and draw the blanket up over her instead.

She grabs my wrist. "Stop being so stubborn. You need to sleep, or you're going to collapse."

Her touch is exhilarating and agonizing at the same time. My cock throbs, threatening to break free of my modesty shield. Yearning to discover her secret warmth. If I stretch out beside her... I gently free my wrist from her grasp, eyes locked with hers. "If I'm next to you, I can't rest."

Tension coils between us. Then her cheeks darken and understanding dawns in her eyes. "Oh," she says on a breath that makes my cock throb with need.

BETHANY

At first I think Izhima means he wants the cot to himself, but then his gaze drifts down my body with what I can only assume is longing. I gulp, heat flooding through me and concentrating in my core. Once my body is pressed against his, I'll probably want to do anything but sleep, too. I work to keep my voice from trembling as I offer, "We could have a quickie to relax."

His eyes flash, and ever so slowly, he cups my cheek and runs the pad of his thumb across my lips. My breathing shallows, and every inch of my skin tingles with desire for his touch. I open my mouth to draw his thumb in, but he pulls away.

"A quickie would not be enough with you, especially… with your amnesia." His voice is deep and sexy and makes me want to melt like chocolate. But what's with the strange pause?

His concern for me only makes me want him more. To lose myself and escape from this horrible situation, even just for a moment. I grab his wrist again. "Please.

I'll do all the work. I just… I need to feel something else."

He releases a slow breath, his dark eyes somehow darker. Then he seems to reach a decision. He slides beneath the blanket and pulls me against him, my skin still sensitive but no longer painful. His breath drifts across my cheek, then he feathers his lips over mine. My eyes close automatically and I inhale his masculine scent, tilting my chin up slightly. When his lips close over mine in a full-blown kiss, his mouth is firm yet incredibly soft, his tongue sliding easily between my lips.

Remembering that I promised to do all the work, I loop my arms around his neck, preparing to roll myself on top of him. But he pushes me back against the mattress, one hand beneath my jaw as he deepens the kiss and wedges a knee between mine to lie half-atop me. Every inch of my skin fires to awareness against his body as he plunders my mouth, tongue driving in and out as if he wants to consume me.

I've been daydreaming about kissing him all day, trying to dredge up a memory of our previous intimacies. This kiss is everything I dreamed of and more. Supple, heated, and singing with passion. Our tongues spar for long moments before his lips leave mine, gliding to the space beneath my ear. "You realize the crew could be watching."

I'm panting, hands roving his shoulders and biceps, yearning for more as my eyes pop open to the dim surroundings. It makes sense the ship might have cameras. I search the dark corners of the room for a telltale red light. Nothing. But alien surveillance is probably nothing like human tech.

Regardless of whether or not there are cameras, I don't want Izhima to stop what he's doing. I need this. I need him; to feel him move inside me. Pulling the blanket up over his shoulders to cover us, I slide my hand lower, fingertips skimming his muscular ass. I murmur, "They can't see anything under the blanket."

Izhima's breath is hot against the side of my throat. He makes a low, sexy noise. "You're used to getting your own way, aren't you?"

I think he's right, and I don't plan to make an exception to that now. "Yes, I am," I reply as I thread my fingers in the back of his hair and bring his mouth back to mine.

He kisses me deeply, supporting his weight on one elbow. His rigid cock is a throbbing rod against my thigh. I throw my free leg up over his hip, trying to pull him all the way between my legs, but he doesn't budge. His hand leaves my neck to slide over my collarbone to my breast, fingers kneading through the fabric. I flinch, my skin still over-sensitive, but I don't want to complain.

Not that I need to. He's in-tune with my reactions and moves on, touch feather-light as he grazes along my hip. With agonizing slowness, he rucks up the hem of my dress, reaching behind the leg I have thrown over his hip. Delightful shivers flutter through my core as he traces light fingertips up the back of my thigh toward my ass. He dips between my legs, grazing the lace panties covering my sex.

A moan escapes my lips as he strokes back and forth over the growing dampness. I arch my back, rocking in time to his gentle yet firm probing. The tension inside me builds with delicious intensity. But soon I need more. Before I can ask, he slides beneath the lace and finds my slick folds.

I moan as he slides between my lips and circles my opening, sending my wetness flooding over his fingers. Up and down, teasing my lips and clit, circling the opening to my channel with sweeping strokes that almost bring me to climax.

His hips are flexing in time to his strokes, rigid cock rubbing against my thigh. I want to touch it, to wrap my fingers around the heated shaft and draw him to me, into me. But his wide shoulders are in the way. All I can do is lie there and let him pin me with his kisses and explore my pussy with his fingers. He slides one thick digit inside me, and I moan into his mouth. His finger pumps in and out shallowly.

I arch, wanting more, wanting deeper. The angle isn't quite right. After a few more strokes, I can't stand it anymore and drop my leg from his hip, opening myself to him from the front.

In one sure move, his finger plunges into me, thicker and hotter than I ever imagined a finger could be.

With a cry, I buck up into his palm, fingers digging into his shoulders. He quickly resumes his previous rhythm, only this time inside me. His tongue draws dizzying circles over my throat. He seems to know my body well, adjusting pressure and rhythm. I'm going to come if he keeps this up, and I haven't even touched his cock yet.

I let go of his shoulder and move a trembling hand down his chest and abs toward where his cock is pinned between us. He's been subtly flexing his hips, pumping against me. My hand reaches his lower abs, thrilled at the rippling flex of his muscles, but he doesn't let me slide between us to touch him.

"I want to feel you," I murmur, nearly out of my mind at the rockets of pleasure tingling along my thighs. My panties are soaked through, and wetness slicks my thighs as he strokes faster, still not giving an inch to my questing fingers.

He plunges inside me relentlessly, though, until my breath hitches and my legs shudder. I gasp and pant, dizzy under his touch, bucking up against him, mindless in my need for release. My orgasm bursts like fireworks behind my eyes and rolls through my body like a storm.

"Izhima!"

He swallows my cries of ecstasy with kisses, continuing to drive into me with his fingers until every pulse of pleasure has been pulled from my aching body.

10

IZHIMA

*P*leasing Beth is like a drug. I want to make her come again and again, to make her cry my name until her voice grows hoarse. I planned to satisfy her enough to keep up the ruse that we are mates, but now both of my shafts are so hard I think they're about to shatter. Holding her close, I wait for her breathing to even out. Now that she's satisfied, I imagine she'll be ready for sleep and I can withdraw.

Instead, she wedges a hand into the non-existent space between us toward my crotch. "Your turn."

Just like her compliments to my food, her unexpected attentiveness to my needs takes me off guard. I catch her hand, kissing the palm before cradling it against my chest. Much as I want to accept her offer, I know if we continue our intimacy, it won't stop at mutual masturbation. "Next time," I say, voice low and gruff. "We're both tired."

Her guilt is heavy against my *Iki'i*, but so is her exhaustion. "But—"

"Please, for once don't argue." I pull her tightly against me and kiss her temple.

She sighs. Though her guilt remains solid, a tinge of relief lightens the air. Within seconds, her breathing evens out in slumber.

I close my eyes, trying to find my own peace. My balls ache, and my blood is on fire. Her body is half thrown over mine, her head nestled in the crook of my shoulder, and the smell of her sex perfumes the air. I could slip away and relieve myself with her none the wiser, but I don't want to leave. I close my eyes and try to find rest, even if I know sleep is impossible.

BETHANY

I wake on my side with one arm and one leg draped over Izhima's warmth. My head is still pillowed on his biceps, his hand loosely curled around my back and ribs. The bay is dim, and I'm warm and comfortable, so

I try to find sleep again, but my mind is spinning, and my eyes just won't remain shut.

I open them a crack and examine Izhima's profile; smooth brow without that Cro-Magnon look some women are into, the perfect nose to chin ratio, sensuous lips, and dark lashes. Even his ear is sexy, and I want to lean forward and nibble the lobe. I resist the urge, respecting his need for sleep.

His eyes pop open, and he looks sideways at me. "Why are you awake?"

My heart races. "Why are you?"

"Because someone won't stop staring at me."

I smile softly. "I can't help it. You're beautiful."

His brow furrows, and the arm beneath my head stiffens. "Are you trying to insult me?"

I blink, confused. "Why would you think that?"

"Humans don't use that term for males."

I chuckle. "We do if it's true." I hadn't thought about him being alien in a while now. He'd become just Izhima, the man who took care of me. The man I'd fought with and dragged into this mess. The man who'd rescued me. How many arguments had we gotten into because of cultural misunderstandings like this one?

I wiggle closer and rub my nose around the shell of his ear before settling my cheek against the pocket of his shoulder. "You smell good, too."

The arm around my back relaxes, settling against my ribcage once more. "Sleep, *tekina*. It will be morning soon."

But I can't sleep now. I have too many questions. "You said we had a fight about my birthday cake. What was I upset about?"

"You insisted the recipe I used was wrong."

I recall my joke about cake being the most important meal of the day and him thinking I was serious. "What recipe did you use?"

"According to my research, cake is a bread-like food made from a dough or batter that's usually fried or baked in small flat shapes and is often unleavened. The humans on the *Romantasy* seemed to enjoy fried items from our menu, so I thought that would please you as well. You were not happy."

Picturing a stack of fry bread with a candle on top, I realize I'd been right—this was a cultural misunderstanding. "Oh, Izhima, I'm sorry. That's actually a funny mistake. I don't know why I'd get upset when all you were trying to do was celebrate my birthday. I guess we haven't been married long, huh?"

After a brief hesitation, he says, "I never said we were married."

My breath catches as I try to process his words. I frown and lift my head to look at him again. "Yes, you did."

"I said you are my mate."

"Oh." Another cultural misunderstanding. "What's the difference?"

He turns to look at the ceiling once more, his body rigid. "Marriage is a choice. Finding one's mate is destiny."

I'm not sure if he's upset or what, but I don't want to start another fight, not now when things seem to be improving. I lower my cheek to his chest again. "Well, marriage is just a piece of paper, anyway. What's important is we love each other."

He clears his throat, as if about to say something, but the lights come on with sudden brightness. The captain's voice comes over a speaker. "Time to make us breakfast, lovebirds."

My fingers curl into a fist over Izhima's heart. "They *were* spying on us."

"As I said," he replies.

I sigh and push the blanket down. As my hand slides down Izhima's stomach, I bump into an erection the size of a summer sausage. *Oh, my.* Still pillowed on his chest, I drop my chin to look. The Speedos of the previous evening are gone, and I'm staring at the most enormous cock I've ever seen. I gulp. *He's still hard?* I really should've insisted on taking the lead last night, though it's hard to believe that would ever fit inside me.

I didn't realize I'd circled my fingers around its girth until Izhima's hand catches mine, drawing it away from his cock. His chest rises and falls rapidly beneath my cheek. "Don't."

The tingling between my legs is almost unbearable. I drag my gaze away from his crotch. "Sorry," I say. I'm going to have to find a way to snag a few minutes without the crew watching so I can fuck my husband—no, my *mate*—silly. "Habit, I guess."

Izhima eases his arm out from under me and sits up, swinging his legs to the floor. His shoulders seem slumped, and his skin still has that ashen look. "We'd better get started."

I frown. "Did you get any sleep at all?"

"The rest I need will have to wait until we're off this ship." He stands, and I see he's once more covered by the Speedos, though they do little to mask the massive bulge underneath.

I sigh. He didn't rest well because he wants to protect me, and I didn't help the matter by giving him blue balls—though to be fair, I did offer to remedy that. I hand him the blanket. "Do you want to wear this so you don't have to spend energy emulating clothing?"

"Thank you." He wraps the rough fabric around his waist, drawing the hem up between his legs and tucking it into the waistband so he looks like he's wearing harem pants.

I shove my aching feet into my heels and we head down the gray corridor to the bathroom—I guess they call it a head on the ship. During our brief visit last night, I was surprised by how clean the facility was compared to the rest of the ship. Turns out aliens *do* have automatic cleaning technology. The crew just hasn't invested in it except for the bathroom, which I'm not knocking, because one less thing to clean, right? I want to gag at the thought of mopping up alien excrement.

The head contains two basins that serve as toilets, dual sinks recessed into the wall, and a single stall that Izhima called a sanitizer. I was too tired to explore using it last night, which might've been a good thing if the crew has us under surveillance. But I feel grimy from my work yesterday, and much in need of a shower. I glance around the plain gray walls. "Do you think they have cameras in here?"

"Perhaps. But you don't need to undress to use the sanitizer." Izhima steps into the stall and pushes a button. He widens his stance and lifts his arms as what looks like steam shoots out of tiny nozzles in the wall, followed by a bar of violet light that circles him. He pushes another button and runs his fingers through his hair as light targets his head. When he steps out, his skin looks a fraction less ashy, and the iridescent blue luster of his dark hair is more vibrant. "Your turn."

11

BETHANY

I step inside cautiously. It smells weird in here, like ozone and coffee, but better than my own sweat. Having serious doubts about this thing actually working, especially if I don't remove my clothes, I push the same button Izhima used and spread my arms and legs. Mist fills the stall, permeating my dress and warming my skin. I expected it to be moist, but it doesn't give me any sensation at all, nor does the light that follows. I'm not sure if it's safe to inhale the mist, so I hold my breath until I'm forced to gasp for air. When the light goes off, my skin feels refreshed, and I can no longer smell myself over the coffee-like scent. Even my dress is clean, the smudges from my work yesterday erased from the fabric. *Nice.* Dry cleaners could make a killing with one of these contraptions back home.

Step one complete, I push the next button and run my fingers through my shoulder-length curls while light plays through the strands. The knots come loose with ease, and the strands lose the oily, tacky feeling they have when they're dirty. When the light goes out, I don't feel nearly as good as I do after a shower, but I feel cleaner, even under my dress where I was the most worried.

I step out of the stall, wondering if it might be worth carting the dishes down here after a meal and letting the sanitizer do the work for us. As we head down the corridor to the galley, I loop my arm through Izhima's. The meal Izhima made last night lingers in my mind, and I hate to admit my stomach rumbles for more. "What do alien garbage collectors like best for breakfast?" I ask.

We round the corner to find Choq sitting on a bench, pink claws drumming the tabletop. "Where have you been? I'm hungry and have work to do."

I scowl at the lizard man. "Nebula quality meals take time to prepare, you know."

"I don't have time to wait." Choq stands, lizard features hardened by a scowl.

"Hold on." Izhima moves around me to the drop-down cupboard and comes back holding a tall, thin glass. He sets it on the table in front of Choq. A smell that reminds me of mango and cloves drifts in my direction as he pours something into it from a black jug. "There will be food soon. Enjoy this *zhikegi* while you wait."

Grinning, Choq slowly lowers himself back onto the bench, and takes a thick glug. Izhima must've prepared whatever that stuff is last night.

I hurriedly set more dishes on the table while Izhima programs the replicator. I wouldn't have minded having the kitchen to ourselves for a bit longer, but it's too late now.

Naro and Pjo arrive side by side, followed soon after by the captain. They all sit and begin drinking the *zhikegi* without a second thought. Apparently, they no longer think we might poison them.

Izhima hands me a knife and directs me to cube a hunk of something that looks and feels like raw beef, but smells like strawberries. I'm not sure if I should feel disgusted or hungry as I slice through it.

Drizzling a vinaigrette over a bowl of something that looks like robin eggs, Izhima sets the first course on the table. The crew chats while they eat, mostly about shipping lane logistics and the value of various items they've discovered in the refuse. Someone at the table belches, and Pjo laughs.

I focus on chopping and stirring and whatever else Izhima directs me to do. The crew devours the various dishes Izhima provides. When they're done, the captain says, "Female, you'll start cleaning my quarters first today."

"As soon as we've eaten and cleaned up in here," Izhima says.

"Very well." The captain rises, followed by the rest of the crew.

As soon as everyone has cleared out, I sigh and plop exhausted onto a bench. Izhima sits across from me and hands me a plate. I've snitched a few nibbles of food while we prepared, but my stomach feels like a hollow pit. I don't even worry about whether or not the crew has touched the food before I help myself to the leftovers.

I start with a sip of the *zhikegi* drink, which tastes a bit like mango but is more bitter and delivers a kick like caffeine. Then I select something that looks like a sticky bun and take a bite. Nutty and sweet and melt-in-your-mouth delicious. "God, that's good."

Izhima's dark eyes focus on my mouth as I lick the stickiness from my thumb and finger.

A lump fills my throat and I freeze. "What? Should I not eat with my fingers?"

He quickly turns his attention to his plate and picks up his own sticky bun. "You're fine."

Suddenly self-conscious, I pick up my eating utensil and stab a blue egg thingy. It has a creamy, fishy flavor I don't care for, but it isn't terrible, so I finish it, not wanting to be rude. "So I guess I'm supposed to clean the captain's quarters first today."

"I'll go with you."

I frown. "Don't you need to prep for lunch?"

"I told you I'm not letting you wander this ship alone. You'll help me cook, and I'll help you clean."

I smile at him gratefully and gather the dishes into a portable tub. "I'm going to take these to the head and see if that sanitizer thing can work its magic. That could make our job go faster."

He raises his eyebrows, then nods slowly. "That's not a bad idea."

Once I've gathered everything and wiped down the table, he helps me carry the basket to the head. We set everything on the floor of the sanitizer and turn it on. I assume it's going to take a little time to eradicate the food grime, so I put my arms around Izhima's neck and draw his face down to mine, smiling into his eyes. I've been thinking a lot about our time together last night. "We should have a little time if you want to, uh…" I slide a hand down his chest toward his groin, "get anything out of your system."

His hands creep to my waist, yet he stands rigid. "We'd better not."

"Well, tonight you'd better be ready, because I'm going to make it all about you." I rise onto my tiptoes and brush my lips over his.

He groans and closes his eyes. "There's something I need to tell you—"

Someone clears their throat behind me, and I twist to see Choq in the doorway. He holds something green and sparkly in his claws. "I think this belongs to you."

It's a cell phone. I recognize the image on the screen immediately—a selfie of me and my sisters, Suzanne, Jennifer, and Tamara.

In a rush, all my memories come flooding back.

12

IZHIMA

"Izhima, I remember everything!" Beth grabs my hand, her eyes glinting with elation. But her joy is a mere flash of blue sky ahead of a coming storm, quickly swept aside by shock and confusion. She takes an unsteady step backward. "Wait." Her eyes narrow to slits. "You lied to me!"

My chest feels tight. I don't like the sense of betrayal I see in her eyes. This isn't how I wanted her to regain her memories. I reach for her hand again. "Beth—"

She recoils from my touch. "It's Bethany." Snatching the phone from Choq's clawed grip, she clutches it against her chest. "Not Beth. Bethany."

"What's going on?" Choq asks, watching us from the doorway. Like all Qalqan, his emotions are closed to me, but I'm worried he's poised to exploit any opportunity that presents itself.

"Give us some privacy, please." I shove the crewman backward into the hallway and cycle the door closed. I knew it wouldn't be easy to explain things when Bethany got her memory back, but I didn't expect an explosion like this. Turning back to her, I mutter, "Keep your voice down."

But the rage churning inside her is like a battering ram. "No, you keep your voice down! You made me believe…" she chokes on the words, and her attention slides down to my crotch. "I almost…"

Eyes blazing, she reaches for the door control, but I grab her wrists and shove her backward against the wall. "Remember what happened the last time you hit a button without thinking, Beth?" I purposefully use the name she asked me not to use, hoping it reinforces the idea that we're supposed to remain in character. "Don't do something we'll both regret."

Wrenching one hand free of my grip, she slaps me across the face. The stinging blow echoes against the bare walls.

I remain perfectly still, keeping my gaze locked with hers. Perhaps I deserved that. Perhaps I didn't. But now isn't the time to argue. I lean closer. "Your recklessness is going to get us both killed." I direct a look at the door, assuming Choq is eavesdropping on the other side. "Turn down your indignation before you blow the lid off this kettle."

She shakes her head hard enough to send her auburn hair flying around her face, but some of her ire subsides. When she speaks again, her voice is low. "We barely know each other. And you… you took advantage of me."

Now it's my turn to fight back indignation. "I suggest you rethink that. You asked me—begged me—to touch you."

To my satisfaction, her cheeks redden. And *kuzara* if I don't want to touch her again right now.

BETHANY

It's all I can do not to shout at him, but I force my voice to remain low. "You never should've let things go that far."

My face is on fire, but I can't deny that I'd insisted on his touch. I barely know him; I'm not even sure I like him after all this. How could he have led me on like this?

"We're both lucky I stopped when I did," he says through clenched teeth. "A Kirenai's mating instinct is not to be taken lightly."

Mating instinct? I gulp and remember his rigid cock pressed against my thigh. How badly I'd wanted to touch it, to stroke him until he came all over me. To open my legs wide and let him fill me with pleasure. My gaze slips downward to the blanket still fastened around his hips. Is that an erection I see under the thick fabric? Against every sane thought, I feel hot wetness flood my panties. Lord help me. Despite everything, I still want him.

Letting out a long breath, I drag my attention back to his face. I don't want to think about how sexy he is right now. Or imagine his body pressed against mine.

I want to be angry.

I want to rant and cry over the hot mess we're in. The trouble *I* got us into. Now that those last moments on board the *Romantasy* have returned, I need somewhere else to focus my blame. "Why the hell was there a button in that kitchen that would eject us into space? That seems like a major design flaw."

Izhima arches an eyebrow. "There was a warning sign."

I sort of recall some alien squiggles posted near the button, but I assumed it was just a reminder to keep the cooler door closed or something. "What about those of us who can't read alien?" I toss my hair, feeling more justified with every passing second. "That button was an accident waiting to happen."

"Which is why you weren't supposed to be in there." He crosses his arms, eyebrow still raised. "And you refused to listen when I told you to stop."

Well, shit. I can't argue with that. My shoulders slump, and my temper fizzles like flat champagne. Slowing down and being rational has always been a challenge for me. If you slow down, you get dismissed and ignored. Yet even I can't deny that sometimes slow and steady wins the race. *Or keeps you from ejecting yourself out an airlock.*

I bite my bottom lip, remorse clogging my throat. "Point taken."

His shoulders relax slightly, and he looks at me warily.

This argument is going nowhere. I know he lied to protect me from being gang raped by this lecherous crew. He kept me in the dark because he didn't trust me not to blow our cover. Yet here I am, throwing a tantrum and proving him right. Izhima's gone above and beyond what a normal person would do to protect a perfect stranger. Swallowing my pride, I say, "I'm sorry."

To my surprise, Izhima's eyes soften and he takes my hands. "Well, to be fair, I wasn't supposed to be in that kitchen, either."

His touch reminds me of the way he held me in those terrifying moments we were swept into space. The way he pulled my body against his and wrapped me in his warmth and air. *He risked his life to save me.* Then and now. And I've been little more than a selfish brat. Keeping my eyes on his so he knows I'm sincere, I say, "Thank you for saving me."

Izhima nods slowly. "You can thank me once we're out of this mess. Right now, you need to remember that there are eyes and ears all over this ship. Someone could be listening at this very moment." He glances meaningfully toward the door. "In fact, I'm sure of it."

Sudden alarm freezes my breath. I glance toward the exit. Is Choq standing outside with his ear pressed to the panel? I step closer to Izhima and whisper, "What will they do if they discover our... situation?"

He runs a hand over his dark hair. "Probably eject me back into space and sell you to the highest bidder. Human females are worth a fortune as breeders on the black market."

Breeders? I shudder. "I don't understand why us being mated changes their plans."

"Kirenai mate for life. A mated female can't physically produce offspring with anyone else."

He hovers close for a few heartbeats, looking into my eyes. I think he's about to say more, but someone knocks on the door. "What's going on in there?"

My heart lurches into my throat. The voice is Pjo's, which means Choq probably already reported to the others.

Without warning, Izhima sweeps me into his arms and crushes his lips against mine.

What the hell? I understand we need to pretend we're together, but there's nobody here to watch us at the moment. My hands flutter against his shoulders, caught between pushing him away and falling into the pleasure of the moment.

He deepens the kiss, one arm tight around my waist, the other supporting my head while his tongue delves between my surprised lips. My nipples harden to pinpoints against his chest and my breath comes in panting gasps. His smell is sexy, like toasted almonds with a hint of musk, and I can feel his erection lengthening against my belly.

A moan escapes me just as I hear the door shush open.

"What the fuck?" The captain punctuates the words with a dissatisfied clicking. "This isn't a pleasure cruise."

Izhima releases me, twisting to face the captain while keeping one arm firmly about my waist. "Our apologies, captain. Just making up after a lover's spat. We'll get back to work."

Like vultures, the rest of the crew hovers in the corridor behind the captain, gawking over his spiny shoulders at us. Naro asks, "What are our dishes doing in the shower?"

"It's a sanitizer, idiot." Choq slugs him in the shoulder.

The onyx-skinned crewman scowls. "Why didn't I ever think of that?"

The captain turns and points down the corridor. "Everyone get back to work. There's a refuse cloud on the sensors a few clicks ahead, and I expect there'll be competition, so everyone get ready." Turning buggy eyes back toward us, he says, "I catch you loitering again, and the deal's off."

I nod, still dazed from both the kiss and everything that's happened. Izhima, however, seems completely composed. He steps away to retrieve the tub of dishes from the sanitizer. "We'll start on your cabin as soon as we get these put away."

Clicking his mandibles, the captain pivots and stalks down the corridor.

My legs feel wobbly without Izhima's arms holding me up, and I feel stupid for letting his acting get to me. He must've planned for us to get caught kissing, but damn, he does a good job making our attraction feel real. I need to stop letting my hormones run wild and focus on the task at hand.

That thought sobers me slightly, and I glance at the dishes, curious if the sanitizer worked. They look sparkling clean, and I breathe a sigh of relief. One less disgusting chore to handle. But it also means we have to clean the captain's cabin now. I can only pray it's not as grimy as the cargo bay or the galley.

As we leave the lavatory and make our way down the dingy gray corridor, I realize I've been missing for at least two days now. My sisters are probably going absolutely bananas with worry.

"Losing two people out of an airlock must be generating a ton of bad press for the cruise line," I say as we round the corner into the galley. "Do you think there's any chance a rescue team will track us down before we reach a port?"

Lips pressed into a grim line, Izhima opens a cupboard and starts stacking dishes. "Nobody is looking for us. If they even discover what happened with the airlock, they'll believe it's too late to save us."

I grip an empty pot, feeling like a boulder just lodged itself in the middle of my stomach. "So nobody's searching? Not even for our bodies?"

He shakes his head. "Space is vast, and we're not high enough profile to warrant the manpower."

Trying my best not to tremble, I shove the pot into an empty space on a shelf next to something that resembles a glass bong. "I wish I could let my sisters know I'm okay. They must be insane with worry." I pull my phone from where I'd stashed it inside my bra, hoping some miracle has given me reception. Instead, I see my overdue birthday celebration reminder pop up on the home screen. My heart feels like it shrivels inside my chest. In a small voice, I say, "Oh, no. I missed my birthday."

Izhima looks at me with a worried expression. "What happens to humans who miss a birthday?"

I try to shrug off my disappointment. "Nothing, I guess."

But I can't help wondering if I'll ever get to celebrate a birthday with my sisters again.

13

BETHANY

*I*zhima and I enter the captain's cabin, and I feel like I just stepped inside an old charcoal grill. It's not hot, but dark soot covers every surface—from the bed at the back of the quarters, to the knick-knacks on the inset shelves, to the tall, round table where the captain is sitting. He's studying a holographic screen with symbols I can't read. Just beyond him, a small round viewport looks out onto the stars, the first view of the outside I've seen since coming on board. It reminds me of that terrifying moment when we were blasted out of the airlock, and I turn my gaze away with a shudder. Cleaning the cabin is going to be horrible in more ways than one, I can tell already.

Izhima steps past me, his bare feet kicking up small puffs of black dust, and I take a step back, covering my mouth and nose. "Is it safe to breathe in here?"

The captain frowns. At least, I think he's frowning. His mandibles are turned down like a malformed mustache, and his buggy eyes are narrowed.

Izhima reaches for my hand and pulls me inside next to him. "Forgive us, captain. We didn't realize you were female."

Female? I blink at the captain, trying to determine why Izhima thinks that. Is it because of the soot? God, what the hell is this stuff? I gulp and ask, "Will one of you please tell me why everything's black?"

Izhima points toward a ceiling corner. "G'naxian symbiote dew."

I squint toward the corner and make out what appears to be a forest-green, winged beetle about the size of a dinner plate clinging to the wall. Another shudder runs through me; I'm pretty sure dew is just a polite term for feces.

The captain clicks three times, each sound deeper than the last. Sadness? "I have no younglings to lap it up."

"My condolences," Izhima says with genuine feeling.

I don't understand, but my sister's chihuahua means the world to her, and she loves to talk about it, so I ask, "Does your symbiote have a name, captain?"

The captain blinks at me like an owl, one eye at a time. "G'lurr."

I can't tell, but I think she may be pleased that I asked. "Great name! My sister has a pet too. A dog we call Beanie. He's not much bigger than G'lurr."

The captain's spines flare, jutting from her head and shoulders like the crest on a bird.

Izhima nudges me and speaks in a soft voice. "A symbiote isn't a pet. It produces a substance used to feed G'naxian infants."

My heart constricts, and I look at the captain with fresh eyes. This dew stuff is their version of baby formula. Did she lose a baby? Why else would the symbiote be producing so much? And why is it spread all over the damn room? Much as I want to ask all these questions, I decide to save them for later, when Izhima and I are alone. The last thing I want to do is offend anyone more than I already have.

I bow my head. "You have my condolences as well."

The captain's spines sink back into their usual positions, and she turns her attention to Izhima. "It will displease my crew if the midday meal's late. Go back to the galley. Your mate can clean here without you. I will bring her to lunch with me."

My heart threatens to beat its way out of my ribcage. Female or not, I'm not comfortable being alone with her. I glance desperately toward Izhima.

Without meeting my gaze, he presses his lips into a tight line and nods. "Yes, captain."

I gape at him. He's been so insistent about not leaving me alone, and although the captain has been the most neutral of the crew when it comes to my role on board, she still threatened to sell me on the black market. I open my mouth to argue, "But—"

Izhima squeezes my hand to silence me and leans over to kiss my cheek. "You'll be fine." Then he marches from the room.

I watch the door swish closed behind him. It feels like he took all the air with him. How could he abandon me like this? Unprepared, unprotected, and completely out of my element. I spin back toward the captain, broom handle gripped tightly in both hands.

She's watching me like a kid glued to a cartoon on TV. A shiver runs down my spine. I'm alone with the captain of a crew who wants to rape me.

IZHIMA

I take a deep breath and let it out slowly as I head to the galley. I feel stupid for not recognizing the captain as female, though with G'naxians it can be difficult to tell. She's not what I'd consider an ally, but she's also less of a threat than I previously assumed, and my *Iki'i* sensed no ill intent when she told me to go. Bethany will be safe in her cabin with her while I prepare lunch. And it gives me a chance to do something special for Bethany's birthday.

Her disappointment when she mentioned she'd missed the event is still lodged like a splinter in my *Iki'i*. Kirenai don't celebrate birthdays, but it seems humans think observing the day is important, and with everything that's happened, the least I can do is try to honor this one small thing. I've stopped trying to deny that she's truly my mate, that beneath our ruse is an even stronger truth. Each interaction between us confirms my feelings. Despite my moments of frustration, I've come to realize she isn't selfish as I first thought. Just passionate and impulsive—traits I can even appreciate much of the time.

I rummage through the cupboards for ideas about what to make. I know better than to try making a cake again, not until she shows me what a birthday cake should be. But I'm determined to make her something special.

Someone clears his throat behind me, and I turn to see Pjo leaning against the edge of the doorway. The Klen's eyestalks swivel, taking in the room. "Where is your female?"

Though I think Bethany is safe alone with the captain, I'm not confident the captain would exert much effort to defend her against the crew, so I keep my answer vague. "Cleaning another part of the ship."

"Mmm." Pjo looks over his shoulder down the corridor, and for a flicker, I wonder if I'm going to have to abandon my cooking to follow him. But then he returns his attention to me. "How long have you been mated?"

"Not long." I know he's trying to catch me in a lie, and I'm not going to give him an opening. I turn back to the cupboards, forcing myself to seem unconcerned but keeping my *Iki'i* wide open for any change to the Klen's mood.

"Have you met a lot of humans? What are they like?"

I hate to admit she's the only one I've spent real time with, so I say, "The emperor only recently opened Earth to the Consortium, so there haven't been a lot of opportunities. But I'll say the ones I've met are... interesting."

Pjo chuffs an appreciative laugh. "So you got to try a few on for size before settling on this one?"

I glance over my shoulder to see him making a lewd stroking motion with one hand. Not liking where this conversation is going, I turn to look him fully in the eyes. "I know that Kirenai are considered promiscuous by some, but that doesn't mean we don't respect each and every partner we take."

He drops his hand, eyestalks twitching. "If you didn't try a few, how can you know this female is really your mate?"

Ah, now I understand. He's trying to get me to admit that a mate bond might not have formed, but I won't fall for that trap. "A Kirenai mate bond is not just about sex. It's a connection between two people that goes deeper than anything you can possibly understand. Mates can recognize each other without ever having sex."

Pjo says nothing for a moment, and I think he's given up. But then he says, "You get frustrated with her a lot. And Choq told me he found out you lied to her."

My heartbeat kicks into overdrive. How much did Choq overhear? I don't think he came to any definitive conclusions, but it's obvious the crew is suspicious. Again, I try to be nonchalant. "Just because we're mates doesn't mean we don't argue." I shrug. "But we always make up."

Pjo runs a glistening tongue along his wide upper lip and takes a step into the galley. "I know we got off to a bad start, but I'd be willing to cut you in on the deal, you know. You can make a few easy credits and wipe your hands clean of this entire messy enterprise. Just say the word."

Disgust sweeps through me toward this being who would so willingly enslave another. In two swift steps, I have him by the throat and am backing him into the corridor. "If you ever talk about my mate like that again, I will break you."

He chokes and sputters, grappling at my hands until I finally release him. We both stand there glaring at each other for a moment. Then he makes a disgusted grunt, turns on his heel, and stalks away.

I return to the kitchen and quickly put together the meal. I need to reinforce my claim on Bethany so the crew has no doubts that we are mated. But how?

BETHANY

I ignore the black dust puffing up as I sweep, trying to ignore the captain's unnerving stare. I still can't believe Izhima left me alone with her, but I have to trust he knows what he's doing.

Movement catches my eye, and I pause to watch the green bug skitter over the ceiling and drop onto the captain's shoulder. It finds a spot between her spines and settles down. I think it's watching me as intently as the captain is.

I smile tightly to cover up how uneasy I feel. My dustpan is full already, and I wonder if I'm supposed to throw it away or keep it. "What should I do with this?"

The captain stands and opens a tip-out panel in the wall near the door. "In here."

I empty the dustpan and go back for more, realizing it's going to take forever to clean this way. "Is there a vacuum cleaner on board?" I ask, then clarify, "A floor cleaner?"

The captain crosses her arms. "If we had an automatic cleaning unit, I wouldn't have assigned you the job."

I let out a shaky breath and scoop another mound into the dustpan, breathing shallowly. I don't know if humans have ever been exposed to whatever this substance is, and I'd hate to be the test case for an allergic reaction. "It just seems like there's a more efficient way to do this, even without a robot. On Earth, we have canisters people push around to suck up dirt."

Continuing to watch me with unnerving focus, the captain asks, "Has your mate spent time on Earth?"

Oh, shit. We're delving into personal territory, and I don't want to get our stories crossed if someone asks Izhima the same question. I decide the best answer is as close to the truth as possible. "No, we've only spent time on ships. We haven't been together long."

"My mate and I weren't together long, either." Sitting back on her stool, the captain clicks three times, the same sound she made when she said she had no younglings. I'm pretty sure it shows sadness.

I bite my lip. "What happened?"

"A captain who doesn't keep the crew happy doesn't stay captain for long."

I ponder her strange answer. "Was your mate the captain of this ship?"

She nods. "He killed the crewman who challenged him, but died of his wounds soon after. The position of captain fell to me by default. But the crew are hard men, difficult to control."

I gulp. She's warning me that Izhima and I are balanced on a very thin blade. I remember Izhima's warning that they'll jettison him back into space if they find out we're not actually mated. *And sell me as a breeder.* My gaze flicks toward the bug sitting on her shoulder. I'm dying to know what happened to their baby.

Before I can muster the courage to ask, the captain points toward my middle. "So, when are you expecting?"

Oh, God. She thinks I'm pregnant. Am I more or less valuable if I'm carrying a child? For all I know, aliens are buying human infants, too. I swallow thickly, considering what I should say.

14

BETHANY

*H*oping to capitalize on the captain's maternal instinct, I decide I'm going to lie. I'll have to bring Izhima up to speed, but I think he'll agree with my decision. Pressing one hand over my belly, I say, "It's only the first trimester, so not for a while yet."

The captain taps the table with a pincered claw. "I'll ask Naro if he can put together anything like this vacuum cleaner you speak of."

I repress the triumphant smile that wants to take over my face. I think I just scored empathy points with the captain. "Thank you. That will make this job go much faster."

While the captain speaks into the intercom, I move to the shelves and start dusting. I don't want to appear lazy. The knick-knacks are all weird little statues. One looks like a T-Rex with an extra set of stubby arms. Another looks like a poop emoji with a pair of rabbit ears. The platform I thought was a bed doesn't have any blankets or padding, it's just a wide shelf. Does the captain sleep on this? For all I know, her species doesn't even sleep.

I glance in her direction. She's finished speaking with Naro and has brought up another holographic screen. I'm happy to have her attention somewhere besides me, so I keep working.

I've just finished dusting the shelves and have most of the platform cleaned off when the captain rises. "Time to eat."

I'm tired and more than happy to get out of her cabin. I'd love to wash up before eating, but we pass the lavatory without a second glance, and I'm not about to argue against getting back to Izhima as quickly as I can.

The smell of lunch hits us before we reach the galley, an unfamiliar, savory scent that makes my stomach rumble. We round the corner to discover the rest of the crew already seated.

Izhima meets my gaze with a question in his eye.

I shrug slightly in response. Everything went okay with the captain, and now that I think of it, I'm less afraid than I was before.

Moving to the sink, I wash my face and hands, cleaning my arms all the way up to my elbows. Izhima is already delivering dishes to the table by the time I finish. Though I'm tired, I ask, "How can I help?"

"Sit down and eat, *tekina*." He puts a hand against my lower back and guides me to the spot next to the captain. "I'm sure you're exhausted."

I smile at him, my heart swelling. I need to ask him what *tekina* means. If I didn't know he was putting on an act, I'd swear he actually cares about me. I settle in and look at a big bowl of what looks like grass in the middle of the table.

Naro is already munching away, sauce dripping from the blades on his spork. He speaks around a mouthful. "I rigged up a suction canister and hose, captain. What do you want me to do with it?"

"Bring it to my cabin after lunch." The captain helps herself to some grass, then nudges the dish my way.

I can't help but grin. A vacuum will make working here so much easier. I don't know why these aliens haven't thought of it themselves, other than I doubt they'd bother to push around a vacuum any more than they do a broom. I place a small mound of grass on my plate and sniff. It smells sort of garlicky with a hint of thyme.

"What's the suction canister for?" asks Naro.

"It'll make cleaning the ship easier," I say, taking a bite of what I've decided is an alien salad. The texture is more like seaweed than grass, which at first seems gross but grows on me as I chew.

"Why are we spending time making things easy for them?" Pjo asks the captain. "So they can keep us up all night rutting in the cargo bay?"

The salad sticks in my throat, and I'm terrified to look at the faces around the table. Had I really been that loud? I didn't think so, which meant Pjo had probably been watching us on camera. I raise my eyes to glare at him, gripping my spork like a weapon. "Don't you have anything better to do than spy on us?"

Pjo's wide mouth twists in a smirk as he focuses one eyestalk in my direction. "Gotta keep an eye on our goods."

I get the feeling he's talking about more than the stacks of junk in the cargo bay, but I refuse to be daunted. "If you're so worried about your precious garbage, then why don't you sleep in the cargo bay and let us have your quarters?"

The captain pushes her empty salad plate aside. "Not a bad idea, all things considered. Plus, a mated couple needs privacy."

Pjo's eyestalks abruptly swivel away from me, and though he doesn't have eyebrows, I'm fairly certain he's scowling. "What?"

"We hired you as a guard. It makes sense for you to keep watch." The captain leans back as Izhima sets a fresh plate of what looks like fat purple pasta on the table. I'm reminded of the squirming dish of worms back on the *Romantasy*, and my already churning stomach threatens to rebel.

"I *was* keeping watch!" Pjo bangs a fist on the table.

The captain emits a sharp click. "Move your things."

Pjo shoves up from his seat. For a moment, he looks like he's going to argue with the captain. Then he turns his glare toward me and stalks from the galley without another word.

I'm not sure if I should be worried or elated. Pjo's angry, but we're also getting our own room. I guess I really did make a connection with the captain while I was cleaning. *Should I thank her?*

Izhima speaks before I can decide. "Captain, we're fine in the cargo bay."

I gape at him. *What the hell?* I just won us our own room, and he's going to turn it down? "Izhima—"

He shoots me a warning look, and with great effort, I swallow my words. I have to trust that he knows best.

The captain waves her empty spork toward the corridor. "Pjo will manage his job just as you are doing yours. He will oversee the cargo. The female will clean the ship."

My elation deflates a little at being called female instead of by my name, but then I realize I don't know her name, either.

Face grim, Izhima grates some black sprinkles onto the purple pasta. "Aye, captain."

Everyone digs in with gusto, but between the tension with Pjo, the strange pasta, and now black sprinkles that look a little too much like the soot I've been cleaning, I've lost my appetite.

I stand and gesture to my seat. "Izhima, you haven't sat with the crew once yet. Why don't you let me serve?"

"Don't worry about me. Sit. Try the *lukulio*. Not as good as fresh, but the replicator did a decent job." He places some of the fat noodles on my plate. Upon closer inspection, however, I realize these aren't noodles or even worms; the purple strands have hundreds of tiny legs along their bodies.

Oh, hell, no. I've tried everything else, but I draw the line at eating centipedes. Besides, I need to prove to the crew that I care as much for Izhima as he does for me.

"Really, Izhima, you need a break, and you're as much a part of the crew as I am. Let me help."

"No." He puts both hands on my shoulders and guides me back onto the bench. "It's your birthday, and I made a special dessert. Not cake, just so you know."

I twist my head and gawk at him. My birthday was technically yesterday—or was it the day before? But the fact he remembered makes me misty-eyed, cake or no cake. "Wow. I don't know what to say. Thank you."

He smiles at me, and the softness in his eyes makes me bite my bottom lip.

"What did you make?" asks Choq, his beady lizard eyes alight with anticipation.

Everyone pushes away their plates, and Izhima sets a tub of lime green sludge in the center of the table. He brandishes a handful of long sticks. "*Ukimi* ice," he announces.

The crew sighs with audible appreciation, and Naro exclaims, "I didn't even know we had *ukimi* sticks on board!"

I'm intrigued as Izhima hands me a stick. It's hollow, like a straw, and seems to be made of some sort of fibrous material with nodules at regular intervals along its length. The crew is looking expectantly at me. Izhima didn't give us separate bowls or glasses, so I look at the straw again. Are we all supposed to drink out of the same bowl? *At least I get to go first.*

I lean forward, about to put my mouth on the end of the straw, when Izhima sits behind me on the bench, lifting me so I'm sitting on his lap. "My bride and I had *ukimi* ice on our first date. Please indulge us in our little ritual."

His cheek is next to mine as he gently grips my wrist and extends the stick toward the tub. I fight back the lovely, fluttery feeling his nearness is giving me and try to relax in his arms, letting him guide me. Breathing in his roasted almond scent, I press my cheek closer to his as he touches the stick to the surface of the bright green *ukimi* with almost sensual slowness. One nodule at a time, he lowers the straw below the surface, dipping it in and out. Once, twice, he drives the stick deeper each time. I find the entire process mesmerizing—sensual, even—as the *ukimi* coats the stick in ever thickening layers.

Despite the crew watching us, my mind is imagining other rods plunging in and out. I swallow and clamp my thighs together under the table to ease the growing desire in my core. My breathing has grown shallow, and I try to keep it normal, but I feel like my hormones just entered a spin cycle. How long is he going to keep this up?

With a sudden flourish, Izhima pulls the stick out. A sparkling green mass that reminds me of cotton candy now encircles the rod. He turns to face me, so close his breath caresses my cheek as he brings the dessert toward us.

"Taste," he says, his voice slightly huskier than usual.

I'm not quite sure how to proceed, so I tentatively stick out my tongue and lick the surface. What feels like foam coats my tongue, and an explosion of tart sweetness fills my mouth, like lemon buttercream frosting but lighter and with a hint of ginger. It almost sparkles on my tongue.

"This is delicious," I say in a low voice, gaze finding Izhima's.

The crew jabs the tub of *ukimi* with their sticks, and within a few minutes, they're all slurping at their misshapen desserts with gusto, oblivious to the green ribbons of *ukimi* dribbled all over the table.

But my attention is still on Izhima. "You didn't have to do this."

He shrugs. "I hope you'll return the favor and show me how to make a cake. I'd like to be on your show."

Warmth fills my chest, and I smile and nod. "I think we can manage some one-on-one baking time." I glance around and give him a sly smile. "Once we're off this ship."

Just then, Pjo bursts back into the galley. He thrusts a froggy finger toward me. "I knew it! This female isn't part of the *Romantasy's* crew. She's a guest." He holds up a tablet with a holographic image hovering above it. A picture of my face. "And according to IDA regulations, the crew isn't allowed to mate guests."

15

IZHIMA

I narrow my eyes at the image of Bethany floating above Pjo's tablet. If he has this, he probably has all sorts of other information as well.

Bethany shrinks back against my chest, trembling in terror. "Where did you get that photo?"

Pjo shoves aside dishes and drops the tablet onto the table. "I hacked into the *Romantasy's* passenger manifest."

I set the ukimi down and wrap both arms around her, keeping my voice low and steady. "Then you also know there were mated guests on the cruise, including the crown prince and princess."

"So why'd you lie and say this female was part of the crew?" Pjo spits out. He turns to the captain. "We salvaged her. That means she's ours. This Kirenai is just trying to steal her so he can sell her himself. Or get a ransom." He rounds furiously on me, his greed like black oil against my Iki'i. "Is she worth a ransom?"

Naro licks green ukimi dribbling from his many-jointed fingers. "Choq said she accused the cook of lying earlier today."

"We'd had an argument, that's all," says Bethany. I'm proud of how steady her voice is, considering how I can feel her trembling in my embrace. "Just because we're mates doesn't mean we always agree."

"This is true." The captain turns off the tablet. "And she's pregnant already, so worthless to trade. Now, can I please get back to my ukimi before it melts?"

I pause on an inhale. *Pregnant?*

But before I have time to process that new bit of information, Choq shakes his head. "Pregnant? No, she ain't."

Bethany has gone completely rigid, and this time, her voice has a tremor. "Humans take months before pregnancy shows. And I think it's safe to assume you've never even met a human before, so how would you know?"

I groan inwardly. This is going to end badly, I can tell.

"I'm Qalqan," Choq says with a toss of his muzzle.

"What does that have to do with it?" she says, some of her usual fire returning.

I lean down and murmur in her ear, "Qalqans are innately skilled in medicine. He can sense these things."

The captain is staring at Bethany with her mandibles twitching, irritation like salt to my Iki'i.

"Another lie!" crows Pjo, dancing from foot to foot and pointing at us.

I have to salvage this situation before things go any farther. Thinking quickly, I say, "We're only recently mated and have been hopeful for a child. My mate was simply over-zealous when she spoke to you, captain."

Choq rises from his seat and goes to stand beside Pjo. "I'm with Pjo. I say we toss the Kirenai out the airlock and take her for ourselves."

Pjo runs a glistening tongue over his wide lips. "I bet she's as fun as she sounds over the speakers."

Naro remains on the bench, drumming his fingers on the table. "I like having a cook and cleaner."

"Whose side are you on?" Pjo shoves his shoulder roughly.

Naro stands. "My own. If they go, I'm back to galley duty. Besides, you just want to fuck her before we sell her, and I don't relish the idea of your ugly spawnlings swarming all over the ship."

"Oh, so my spawnlings are ugly, huh?"

The two start shoving each other as they argue, but my attention is on the captain. Her crest of spines is standing upright, and her mandibles click with every syllable as she looks straight at me and says, "I do not appreciate being lied to."

BETHANY

I tense, certain the captain is about to hand me over to Pjo.

Instead, she rises and gestures a pincered hand toward the door. "I will question you both in my quarters."

Before I even know what's happening, Izhima stands and lifts me from the bench in a single motion, cradling me protectively against his chest. We're striding out the galley door when Pjo spins away from his argument. "Hey! Where do you think you're going?"

"I'll let you know what I decide, Pjo," the captain says.

We reach her cabin without my feet ever touching the floor. Izhima sets me down but keeps one arm around my shoulders as he turns to face the captain.

Instead of opening her cabin door, she points down the corridor. "Keep walking."

Izhima grabs my hand and pulls me along beside him without argument.

"Where are we going?" I glance over my shoulder at the captain, who stalks a few paces behind, her crest of spines bobbing with her gait. "I'm sorry I misled you," I add. "We just really want a baby."

She only clicks at me in return. A few twists of the corridor later, we reach a hatch with a view port looking into a small bare room. A brig? "Stop here," she orders.

We turn to face her, and for long moments she examines us. The silence threatens to suffocate me, but I force myself to remain quiet. I've said too many things wrong already. Down the corridor, I can still hear the crew arguing. The sound of metal clanging against metal rings through the ship, like massive swords in battle, followed by an angry roar. I wince.

The captain says, "I can't have my crew at each other's throats like this."

Remembering her story about her mate, I say, "Your crew is always at each other's throats, whether it's over me or not."

I immediately regret my hasty response. Spines on end, the captain reaches out and opens the hatch. "Be that as it may, I'd rather not add dealing in live cargo to my list of unlawful acts. I'm sending you both out the airlock."

"What?" I gasp, looking into the small room. I can now see that the opposite wall has a second hatch. "But that's murder! Much worse than selling slaves."

Instead of responding, the captain says, "There's another garbage scow in the vicinity." She blinks her eyes one at a time, lowers her spines, and turns her gaze on Izhima. "Are you strong enough to keep her alive for a few hours?"

Dread punches me in the stomach as I realize what she's suggesting. She wants to put us back out in space exactly like they found us, with Izhima wrapped around me to keep me from dying. But I recall the crew saying that protecting me was dangerous for him.

Izhima stands stiff as a block of ice beside me. He even looks pale, and I remember how tired he's been. How much will protecting me demand of him?

He says slowly, "I'm not sure."

The captain shrugs one shoulder and returns her attention to me. "I suppose I'll ask what you prefer, then. Should I keep you, female, or send you both out?"

I can't ask Izhima to put himself in any more danger for my sake. But thinking about what that means for me makes it hard to breathe. I ask, "You could stay alive for a few hours without me, though, right?"

He twists to look at me, a deep crease between his eyebrows. "It doesn't matter. I'm not leaving you."

With every ounce of courage I have, I duck out from under his arm. "You have to. Protect yourself."

His skin flushes a deeper shade of blue. "Never. You're my mate."

I know he's only saying it for the sake of the captain, but the feeling behind his words still sends a shiver up my spine and brings tears to my eyes. I take another step backward. "If we manage to survive, all we're doing is transferring to another garbage ship, and who's to say that crew won't want to sell me, too? Save yourself. If you're alive, you can at least send someone to find me on the black market."

His eyes flash, and he steps forward to lock his arms around me. Turning to face the captain, he asks, "How close is the other ship?"

"Other side of the refuse cloud."

The sound of booted feet echoing through the corridors makes my heart lurch. Pjo's voice calls, "Where'd they go?"

We're out of time. If we're caught standing here, the crew is likely to kill the captain and Izhima both. I shove uselessly against Izhima's chest. "Go now, before it's too late." My breath hitches. "Just… tell my sisters I love them. Please."

"No." Arms around me, he lifts my feet off the deck and steps into the airlock.

I don't even have time to struggle before the captain hits the door control and the hatch cycles closed.

"No!" I look into Izhima's dark eyes. "What have you done?"

A deafening klaxon rises, and blinking, amber light fills the chamber. He presses his forehead to mine. "I love you, Bethany."

That is not what I expected to hear, but I don't have time to respond because the outer door hisses open. For a few brief seconds, gale force wind rips across my skin and we're blown off our feet. Then Izhima's muscular arms and rock-hard chest go soft, and it feels like he pulls me inside of him. I can't move, can't see. Even my lungs feel tight, as if I'm encased in shrink wrap, though I can somehow breathe.

My heart races, and I think of every movie I've ever seen where the hero has to survive under water. *Remain calm*, I tell myself. *Don't use up your oxygen by panicking.* But I can't help it. I'm going to die out here. Izhima's going to die out here. All because of me.

His final words—possibly the last words I'll ever hear— are still ringing in my ears. *I love you, Bethany.*

I can't doubt his sincerity. His actions speak louder than words—he's willing to give his life for me, not once, but twice now. And it might be just another of my impetuous impulses, but I know I love him, too. He's strong, gentle, creative, sexy, and most of all, forgiving. Despite my flaws, my overbearing nature, my rash, impulsive outbursts that are going to be the death of us, he loves me.

And I may never get to say it back.

16

IZHIMA

I harden the protein shell around my matrix, keeping the harsh reality of space at bay with Bethany as a core of warmth at my center. I'm trying not to be pessimistic about our odds of survival as I cycle oxygen from my cells into the tiny pocket of air I've created for her to breathe.

Stars rotate slowly around us as we float away from the garbage ship. The lights from the hull reveal vague outlines of shapes within the refuse cloud, mostly unrecognizable. I make out a broken chair. A misshapen piston from a drone loader. Something that resembles a wad of dirty laundry.

In our wake, the ship twists on its axis, plasma ports firing to hurry it out of sight. We're left in near blackness, the cold light of the stars more backdrop than illumination. My reserves are diminishing faster than I expected, and I search for the telltale lights of another vessel. I see only uncaring stars and unpromising shadows.

Did the captain lie just to get us into the airlock? It's possible. I can't spare the energy to feel emotion about it at the moment.

Something nudges us, setting us spinning a different direction—most likely a bit of flotsam from the refuse cloud. We appear to have reached the garbage field. A grim thought enshrouds my mind. *At least there's a chance someone will find our bodies now.* Bethany would take comfort in knowing her sisters will retrieve her remains.

I don't know how much time has passed before Bethany begins shivering, her body's attempt to create heat, though the action lends little warmth to our cocoon. Her rasping breath grows more shallow. Dread fills me as I'm slowly forced to cut back her oxygen supply. I don't know how much oxygen humans need to survive, but I won't be able to maintain my outer shell much longer if I don't start conserving.

I'm sorry, Bethany. Wrapping my matrix more tightly around her, I hope she can feel what little comfort I have to offer.

One of the stars winks at me. Winks again. I have no energy left to keep it in sight while we rotate, but it looks like the running lights of a ship. Can they see us out here?

The lights grow closer. A beam cuts through the surrounding refuse, searching, searching. *Here!* I think, wishing there was some way to propel myself toward them. But I can do nothing more than float inertly and maintain my shell.

The light sweeps over us once, twice, then remains steady. Elation fills me. Against all odds, we've been found in time. But my joy is short-lived as Bethany's muscle tone goes suddenly limp. Then her breathing ceases altogether. *No!* We only need a few more minutes. I force more oxygen into her lungs. Oxygen I can't spare.

But I will spare it. This will be my last effort. My final breath. Given to my mate.

I can only hope the ship reaches us in time to save her.

BETHANY

I regain consciousness flat on my back, throat parched and skin on fire. *Where am I?* The last thing I recall is

Izhima saying he loved me. Then I realize I'm no longer shrink-wrapped. Full breaths of air rush in and out of my burning lungs.

He did it! He saved us both! I crack open my eyelids to pale overhead lights, elation rolling through me.

A pink lizard face looms into view. I recoil in horror. *Choq?* Did the crew overthrow the captain and recapture us?

"Good, you are awake, human." The alien's voice is gruff, like Choq's, but also more sibilant. His clothes are also different; he's bare-chested except for black suspenders holding up a long black skirt. He presses what looks like a hypodermic gun against the side of my neck, and the burning pain infusing my body subsides.

Not Choq. This is a different lizard man. A different ship. I'm so happy I want to cry.

I turn my head to look around the room. I'm on a cot in what I assume is a medical bay about the size of a single-car garage. On the wall next to me, a holo screen glows with symbols I assume must be my vitals. A hatch stands open to a well-lit corridor, and sterile-looking metal cabinets surround us.

"Where am I?" I rasp, throat still dry.

"This is service vessel one eight six eight." The lizard blinks twice. "We found you floating among some debris. It's lucky you're alive."

Icy dread settles into my bones. "What about my—" I choke over what to call Izhima. My friend? My savior? Then I decide to call him what he is. "My mate?"

The lizard alien pats my hand. "The Kirenai is in our rejuvenation pod. I was uncertain at first that he would recover, but he should be fine."

Relief so strong it threatens to make me pass out again forces me to take a moment just to breathe before I ask, "Can I see him?"

"You need to rest—"

I sit up, my head spinning from the effort. "No. I need to see him right now."

"As you wish." He raises another hypo. "May I offer you a stim before you try to walk?"

"Thank you." I remain still while he presses it into my shoulder. A surge of strength fills my arms and legs. I smile genuinely at him and say again, "Thank you." This spaceship is definitely a step above the last one we were on.

He leads me to a drawer the size of a coffin with more glowing symbols on its front panel. It slides open to reveal what looks like a fish tank full of algae-green liquid with a smell that reminds me of ripe strawberries. The surface ripples as something shapeless and blue moves below the surface.

It looks more like an amoeba than a man. *Izhima?* I hadn't really put two and two together that if he can change form to envelop me completely, his natural state might not look human. But that doesn't matter. What matters is that he's alive. We both are because of him.

"Izhima, I'm here," I whisper.

The surface roils again, and the blue shape at the bottom of the liquid tightens. Then, right before my eyes, it coalesces into the body of a man. Chest, head, broad shoulders, muscular legs. He sits up, shiny green liquid rolling from his shoulders.

Izhima's dark eyes meet mine. "Are you okay?"

I throw my arms around his neck, heedless of the viscous, strawberry-smelling stuff coating his skin. "Yes! I'm okay." Tears prick the backs of my eyes. Then I draw back, looking him over again. "Are you?"

He nods. "Yes. It's a miracle they found us."

I lean against his shoulder again, still not ready to let go. Part of me wonders if the captain somehow informed this ship that we were out there. I may never know, but I send a silent thank you in her direction, anyway.

The lizard doctor—I'm pretty sure now that's what he is—leans down and taps some controls on the edge of the drawer. "I recommend both of you rest longer. We're in the middle of refuse collection, but once we're done, the captain will want to talk to you."

"Can I make a call? I want to let my sisters know I'm okay." I can't imagine what they must be going through since I disappeared. Suzanne is probably trying to rally an armada to search for me, and Jennifer is undoubtedly doing something brainy with her telescope. Tamara... well, who knows with Tamara? She's shy, but I've seen her mama bear come out when it comes to her loved ones.

The doctor bobs his head. "Sorry, no. We're on a tight fuel budget and can't leave the cloud to extend the relay antenna until the refuse collection is complete."

"How long will that be?" Agitation creeps into my tone.

"We had only just entered the cloud when we found you. It will take several more sleep cycles to finish the salvage."

I bite my lip to keep my complaints in check. This crew is in the middle of a job. The least I can do is allow them to finish without incurring extra costs because of me. My sisters can wait a bit longer.

Izhima stands and steps over the lip of the drawer. He's naked, and damn it all, despite the circumstances I can't help noticing how well-endowed he is all over again.

"I will continue my recovery in this form," he says.

The doctor shrugs. "Suit yourself. We have an empty bunk you can use. Come this way."

He escorts us down a corridor that looks like a cleaner version of the previous garbage ship; gray metal with pipes running along the walls, and hatches to either side. One of my high heels has developed a wobble. I'm honestly surprised they've lasted as long as they have, and I mince carefully behind him, wondering if it would be too much to ask for a new set of clothes. But the doctor didn't offer any to Izhima, so I'm not going to push my luck and ask.

Stopping next to an open hatch, the doctor gestures into a narrow room with a bunk on one side of the aisle and brushed metal cabinets on the other. "I'll send someone to get you when it's time for the next meal."

Izhima steps inside and I follow. The door swishes closed behind us, and he glances at the rather small single bed, then at me with uncertainty in his eyes. "One bed."

I stare back, recalling how he gave up the cot to me on the other ship. Does he want me to reciprocate now? Even if we only sleep, I want to be beside him. But what if he's changed his mind? What if he regrets those last words to me?

If there is any time to be impetuous, this is it.

17

BETHANY

It's taking all my willpower not to stare at Izhima's gorgeous chest and abs, let alone his exposed cock. But I need to think about more than sex right now. My feelings are bigger than that, and I have the sense that there will be consequences to what we do next. My heart thumps hard against my breastbone, making it difficult to keep my voice steady. "Did you mean what you said before we went out the airlock?"

He nods slowly, his shoulders remaining stiff. "Yes. I wanted to say it in case we didn't survive."

A flood of emotion clogs my throat, and I press one hand to my chest. I've had several boyfriends, and even told a few I loved them, but none have ever reciprocated, let alone told me they loved me first. I was "too much to handle," most of them said during our inevitable breakup. Yet Izhima isn't trying to backpedal. *He really means it.*

I whisper, "Why me?"

Izhima sits on the edge of the bed and looks at me with a half-smile. "Would it offend you if I said you sort of grew on me?"

I let out a short laugh, my chest still tight. "Give it a little more time. You'll change your mind."

Frowning, he shakes his head. "No, I won't. You might be rash, but you're also funny and smart and sexy." His gaze drifts down my body, still wearing the soiled, worn gown. "And when you let me touch you…"

Just his gaze turns me breathless. I want him to touch me again so badly my body aches. My feelings for him run deep, deeper than for any man I've ever been in a relationship with, despite the fact we've only known each other for a matter of days.

I sit on the bed next to him. I've been accused of being reckless so many times, but what I'm about to say feels more dangerous than jumping out of an airlock. Threading my fingers with his, I say, "I love you too, Izhima."

His fingers tighten, and he licks his lips. I have to struggle not to think about sucking on his tongue. He leans closer, keeping his eyes locked on mine. "I need you to understand what you're getting into. Kirenai mate for life, and if we start this, I won't be able to stop."

I tilt my chin until my lips nearly touch his. "I'm asking you not to."

He lets out a shuddering breath before pressing his mouth to mine. His kiss is reverent, almost chaste. And definitely too slow.

Twisting, I hike up my gown so I can straddle him. I feel like I've waited my entire life for this moment—for a chance to be with him. To have a mate who will love me no matter my flaws or my temper. My hands roam over the peaks and valleys of his bare chest and stomach, pushing him backward onto the mattress with every bit of passion I was forced to restrain on the ship. "It's my turn to please you."

I dip my head to kiss his collar bone, his chest, the hollow between his muscular pecs, reveling in his intoxicating toasted almond scent now mixed with a hint of strawberry and the ever-present lure of his musk. I reach his nipple, a darker blue than the vibrant hue of his skin, and nip it lightly.

He makes a low, throaty sound, fingertips stroking my shoulders and arms. I glance up to see him watching me with dark eyes full of desire, then I move down to the washboard of his abs. He's like a perfect sculpture of corded muscle and smooth skin.

When I reach the tip of his erection, I notice that, while at first glance he'd seemed human, he has some extra parts. Right above his shaft, over his pubic bone, is something that looks like a clit tickler, and below his shaft, right above his balls, is a smaller protrusion, obviously designed for a second penetration. Wetness floods my panties at the thought.

A glistening bead of pre-cum caps his magnificent length, and I run my tongue over the head, lapping up the bead while my hand moves lower to cup his balls. He shudders and groans, fingers threading into my hair. As I roll his balls gently between my fingers, I run the broad side of my tongue along his throbbing shaft from base to head, taking the thick cap into my mouth and circling my tongue around its head.

Relaxing my throat, I take him inside as he flexes upward. I can't fit his entire length without gagging, but I slide up and down, sucking and running my tongue along the underside until his grip on my hair urges me away.

"I want to be inside you."

My pussy is throbbing with need. "Yes."

Standing, I hike my gown up over my head, pulling it free so I face him in only my bra and panties. He sits up and reaches for my hips, pulling me between his knees. His hands slide upward to unclasp my bra. The garment falls from my shoulders and he tosses it aside. With both palms, he caresses my breasts. His cock stands like a flagpole between his legs, and while I enjoy his attention on my breasts, I'm impatient for more.

I thrust my panties down my hips and step out of them. He pulls me closer, sucking a nipple into his mouth as his hand moves down my belly, fingers gliding over my trimmed mound of hair. One thick finger slides between my legs.

I rock into his touch, letting his finger slip between my folds and along my clit. More wetness drips down my thighs. I'm nearly vibrating with the need for release, but his finger won't be enough this time. Pushing him back onto the mattress again, I crawl up his body and look down into his passion-dazed eyes.

His hands find my hips and he pumps upward, grinding his thick length against my outer folds. One hand planted on his rock-hard chest, I tilt to angle him inside, but before I can, he flips me over so I'm on my back. He plants both hands beside my head and looks down into my face. "I need to be sure you want this because there's no going back."

"Shut up and take me," I pant, my hands gripping his firm ass. We've been through enough together for me to know what I want. I want Izhima, now and for always. I try to pull him into me, but he's as unmovable as a hunk of granite.

With the head of his cock poised over my entrance, he lowers his mouth to mine, devouring me in a kiss to end all kisses. Heat, passion, twirling tongues and breathlessness while he pulses against my opening. I buck upward, trying to impale myself on his throbbing cock, but he keeps himself just out of range, only allowing the shallowest of penetrations.

When I think I'm going to die of anticipation, he relents and buries himself inside me with a slow, solid push.

I gasp. He's thick, but not enough to be painful, and he fills me completely. Once he's wholly seated, he pauses, breathing hard. His tickler kneads my clit, and my insides flutter on the edge of an orgasm. I buck up against him, needing him to move, needing him to fill me again and again until I'm driven to oblivion.

"I've imagined this moment since the first day we met," he says, and pulls back. Then he enters me again in sure, quick strokes, no longer pausing but pistoning into me. My juices are slick between us, coating my thighs. I let out a gargled moan as a wave of pleasure rises inside me, crests, and breaks. My orgasm barely ends before another begins to build. He slams forward, filling me, stretching me over and over, the ridges of his cock hitting me in all the right places.

The pressure inside me swells to excruciating heights, a crest I fear might be too high to break. I toss my head from side to side, moaning, "I need," over and over without knowing the answer.

Then he rolls his hips to enter me at a new angle, hands at my neck and shoulder to pin me in place. Something probes my ass—his second shaft, I'd guess. I'm so wet, so aroused, it enters me with little resistance.

I come undone, screaming his name as an orgasm sends me over the edge.

He pumps into me several more times, pushing into both my entrances until his body stiffens and he groans. Heat fills me everywhere, prolonging my orgasm in fluttering waves that take my breath away.

When I can finally breathe again, he's pressing his forehead to mine, panting. "My mate," he says.

I smile up at him. "My mate."

18

IZHIMA

Bethany rests on my chest, cheek pressed over my heart. I love how she feels in my arms, both of us sated from our most recent lovemaking. We've spent the better part of a day and night enjoying each other's bodies, and I'm exhausted, but in a good way. It's fortunate this ship had a Kirenai rejuvenation pod, or I'd never have been able to keep up with my mate's delightfully robust appetite.

She drums her fingertips against my chest in time to my heartbeat. "Izhima, how do you have a heart and other organs if your natural shape is... well, not this one?"

I nuzzle the top of her head, loving the sweet, musky smell of her hair. "Kirenai have major organs just like any living being—heart, lungs, stomach, liver. We adjust them to fit whatever shape we take." I squeeze her tighter, realizing my days of taking on any shape I please are over. I'm glad to discover I don't mind. "But now that you and I are mated, this is the shape I'll have forever."

She lifts her head to look at me. "Does this mean your days of rescuing me in outer space are over?"

I chuckle. "I certainly hope so! But not because I can't do it. I'll still use my resting state—my amorphous form—sometimes. But I can no longer transform to look like another species. This body has settled as a human."

Concern simmers behind her eyes. "Are you okay with that? I'd be upset if I lost my ability to shift into whatever I wanted."

"Absolutely." I smile. "As long as I have you in my arms for the rest of our lives together."

She sighs. "I have trouble believing that."

I roll over, pressing her back against the mattress and kissing her neck. "I'm serious. I consider myself lucky. Some Kirenai go their entire lives without finding a mate. Without even a taste of what it's like to love and be loved. I can never get enough of holding you. Tasting you." I suck the side of her neck gently.

"Stop." She giggles. "You're going to leave me with hickeys."

But I know she loves it because she tilts her head to give me better access. I slide one hand down to give her ass a squeeze and move my mouth lower to one of her nipples. I circle it with my tongue, loving the way it hardens under my attention.

She holds my head to her breast and shivers. "God, you're good at that."

Moving to her other nipple, I nibble the tip gently. "You make me hungry for more."

Spreading her legs, she guides me into her heat with a moan, and soon I'm moving inside her, enjoying the way the friction makes her writhe and buck. She meets my gaze, so full of love that it's all I can look at. Every word I spoke was true: this woman is all that I've ever wanted, and more.

We find ecstasy again in each other's arms, and I lean into her, pressing our foreheads together and gazing into her eyes. Her desire for me is as clear as the love shining there. If I had a choice, I'd be inside her forever, but her stomach growls.

"I'm starving," she says. "Do you think they'd mind if we raid their kitchen?"

I give her taut nipple one more suck, then push up onto my elbows. "I have a better idea. Let's cook the crew a thank-you banquet."

Her eyes light with excitement. "That sounds great." Then her lips quirk into a wry grin. "Maybe I can show you how to make a cake."

I laugh. "It is the most important meal of the day."

My heart soars with joy when she laughs, too.

BETHANY

Izhima gives me one more languid kiss before he stands and opens one of the many cabinet doors in this small room. I've enjoyed the sex—oh, God, have I enjoyed the sex—but I could really use a break, not only because I'm hungry, but because I'm sore in places I never could've imagined being sore.

He pulls out a pair of pants and steps into them. I don't know who they might belong to, but he seems confident he's allowed to wear them. They fit tightly over his muscular ass and thighs like spandex biker shorts with the hem just above his knees. I bite my bottom lip. Good Lord, the sight of his perfectly sculpted ass makes me want him again, soreness be damned.

As if he knows what I'm thinking, he shoots me a sideways smirk. "Shirt or no shirt?"

I swing my feet over the edge of the bed. "You'd better put a shirt on or I may starve to death before we can make it to the kitchen. Any chance there's something in there for me? I dread putting on my gown yet again."

He pulls out what looks like a saffron silk robe. It's buttery soft as I slide my arms into the sleeves and belt it around my middle. He looks me over and makes a low, sexy sound in his throat before he pulls me against his chest. "Mmm. You look good in this."

His hands glide up from my waist to cup my breasts, then around to my ass to pull me against him more tightly. He kisses me, long and hard, until I'm breathless and dizzy.

But my stomach has a mind of its own and grumbles again. He takes a step back and grins. "We'll come back to this later. Let's go eat."

I nod, still dazed and fuzzy with passion as I follow him to the galley.

The layout of this spaceship is very similar to the salvage vessel we escaped from, but the halls aren't choked by the scent of garbage, and the galley is tidy and bright. Izhima sets straight to work, handing me some items to peel and chop, and soon delicious smells are coming from a pan on the stove.

He stirs whatever it is and sets it aside, wiping his hands on a towel. Then he pours us each a glass of hot, sweet tea and offers me a plate of round wafers. I crunch one down as he dips his into the tea. The flavor reminds me of gingersnaps, but with less bite, and when I take another and dip it into the tea, the profile becomes more citrusy. "These are yummy."

"I'll have to make some fresh for you next time," he says. "Though these are fairly decent for prepackaged. Tell me what ingredients we need for your cake. The replicator isn't programmed with any Earth foods, but I'm sure we can work out some equivalents."

I figure a simple pound cake will be easiest, so I list out flour, sugar, eggs, butter, salt, and vanilla.

He comes up with eggs, sugar, and salt easily, then programs several types of flour for me to examine. After I've settled on a blend I think might work, we move on to the other ingredients.

I show him how to whip up a simple pound cake. "Just so you know, this isn't what I'd call a birthday cake," I tell him. "But it's closer than your attempt on the *Romantasy*."

He crosses his arms. "Why do humans have so many versions of this thing called cake? Your Wikipedia lists hundreds, and none of them are the same. Even the specifics on birthday cake only say 'a cake that has various ingredients'."

"I see your point." I place the cake in the oven to bake. "You know, that would be an excellent theme for a show. Not even humans understand how many types of cake there are across the world. And technically, the cake we're making now is completely new because it's using alien ingredients." Another idea nearly sweeps me off my feet, and I grab his hand. "Holy shit, we could do an entire series on that theme alone! Making Earth recipes using alien ingredients! Viewers will eat that up!"

"What's that smell?" A voice at the doorway startles me, and I spin to discover an onyx-skinned alien similar to Naro looking at us. She must be female because she has almost cartoon-like curves, enough to make the slate-gray flight suit she's wearing look like it belongs on a runway model. A small pang of jealousy rolls through me. Her black hair is pulled up on top of her head in a cascade of shiny curls, and her large, dark eyes catch the light in a way that gives them a slight glow reminiscent of embers.

Izhima says, "We thought the crew would enjoy a special meal. It's the least we can do for your efforts to rescue us."

"Oh, how exciting. Just in time for us to wrap up this job." Smiling, she steps into the galley, her gait sultry, hips rolling and shoulders swaying. I wonder if she's trying to be sexy for Izhima, and my hackles rise, but her focus is on me. "My name's Elepa."

"My name's Bethany." I nod. "This is Izhima, my mate," I add, just to make that abundantly clear.

"Oh, believe me, we know." She winks at me and glances briefly toward Izhima before taking a seat at the table.

Heat rises to my cheeks, and I realize I never even considered being quiet while we were in our cabin. "Oh. Sorry."

"No worries." She chuckles. "My mate and I were just as ardent at the beginning of our relationship. Still are, sometimes."

A blue-skinned alien appears in the doorway dressed in a gray flight suit like Elepa's. Though his coloring is like Izhima's, his eyes are much larger, and he has an extra joint on each finger. *Just like his mate*, I realize. He bends to kiss her cheek. "Are you talking about me, *kikajiru?*"

She scoots over on the bench. "Only in the best way."

He sits, looking at me, then at Izhima. "I apologize that I haven't made time to greet you sooner. I'm Captain Arlan. It's good to see you two are recovering."

"A pleasure to meet you, Captain," says Izhima, nodding respectfully. "I'm Chef Izhima Amai, and this is my mate, Bethany Bloom."

"Thank you for saving us," I add.

"We just came out of the refuse cloud and picked up a newscast about you disappearing from the *Romantasy*," says the captain, looking directly at me. "Mind telling me how you ended up in this predicament?"

I grin, my chest aching with love for my sisters. Of course they would've made sure I was all over the news. "I accidentally triggered an airlock in the kitchen," I admit, and quickly explain how Izhima risked his life to save me both from space and the unwanted attentions of the other crew. "My sisters must be sick with worry about me. Can I call them now?"

"I've already informed the authorities, and there is a shuttle on the way, but you can make a call while you wait." He stands. "You'll need to come to the bridge."

Izhima and I follow him down the corridor. I'm nearly dancing with joy at every step and have to restrain myself from racing ahead, despite the fact I have no idea where I'm going.

We reach a ladder and climb up into a cramped space full of control consoles with flickering green lights. A bubble dome overhead shows black space and cold, glittering stars. Where I can see the ship's hull, I also see what look like retractable arms and devices I assume they use to gather the garbage into the ship.

A plump, masculine figure with alabaster skin and cropped blue hair stands at one console. I think he might be human until he glances in our direction and I see his lips are also blue and his face is too flat to be human.

The captain says, "Contact the *Romantasy*, please."

"Yes, captain," says the alien and taps a few commands. Through the bubble dome, what looks like a net extends from the hull, barely visible red lights blinking along the strands. "CLS *Romantasy*, this is service vessel one eight six eight requesting comm access."

I wait impatiently for them to go through protocols, then a blue face with mandibles and spines appears on a view screen in front of the crewman. "This is Captain Zhanuzh of the CLS *Romantasy*."

Unable to control myself any longer, I push forward. "Captain, this is Bethany Bloom. I need to talk to my sisters right away, please. Suzanne, Tamara, and Jennifer Bloom."

The captain clicks. "Of course. They have been awaiting your call."

My sisters appear on the main viewscreen, looking worried but relieved. They press close, their faces streaked with tears as they cry out my name. I break into tears as well. "I knew you guys were looking for me."

"I'm so glad you're safe," says Tamara. Her chihuahua, Beanie, is licking tears from her chin.

"What the hell happened?" Jennifer asks.

Suzanne, however, is glaring past me through the camera. "Is that the alien who kidnapped you?"

I glance over my shoulder to see Izhima with his eyebrows raised, then turn back to the screen. "I wasn't kidnapped. He saved my life." I quickly tell the story of what happened over the past few days, then reach over and grab Izhima's hand, pulling him close. "And I want you all to meet my mate, Izhima."

The lecture I expected about jumping into things too quickly doesn't come. Instead, my sisters grin and give each other knowing looks. Tamara presses one hand against her cheek. "Really? We found mates, too."

Jennifer laughs, and Suzanne says, "I guess they didn't name this ship the *Romantasy* for nothing."

19

BETHANY

*W*e're sitting at a table for eight at the Amorous Starlove Solarium on board the *Romantasy*, having our first evening meal together since my return. Izhima says this is the best restaurant on board, but I have my doubts; the air here smells like a fish market at the end of a hot day.

"Tazhio and I want—" Tamara stops mid-sentence as the small, gray-skinned waiter sets a plate of what looks like green Jello infused with what look like black worms in front of her. "I… thought we were getting salad." She looks like she's about to throw up all over the smoked glass tabletop.

"This is a salad," says the waiter, setting a second plate down in front of Jennifer. "The greens were harvested fresh from the ship's algae farm."

Jennifer pokes the green mass with her fork, setting the mound wiggling. "Are those real worms?"

Tamara makes a choking sound and presses a hand to her mouth.

Her mate, Tazhio, grabs the plate and thrusts it back into the waiter's hands. "Take it back, please. We'll order something else."

"Of course, sir." The waiter scurries away.

Suzanne calls after him, "Bring her some plain crackers, please." She rubs Tamara's back. "Saltines were the only thing that got me through the first few months of my pregnancy."

It turns out my sisters have been having adventures of their own while I was gone; surviving a crash landing, facing down hostile creatures on an alien planet, and finding mates of their own. I can't believe so much has happened so fast, especially that Tamara is going to be a mom.

I poke at my plate of jiggly green "salad" and raise an eyebrow toward Izhima. I'm willing to try most things, but still draw the line at worms.

He's chewing slowly, a slightly disgusted twist to his lips. Shaking his head, he stands and gathers the rest of the dishes. "It seems I'm not the only chef who has trouble preparing human food. I'll be right back."

While he disappears into the kitchen, I turn back to Tamara. "So what were you saying a minute ago?"

She still looks ill, so Tazhio puts one arm around her shoulders and answers for her. "She's ready for the crazy flight that comes with marrying me."

Tamara gives him an affectionate shove. "Spoken like a true pilot." She turns back to us. "I just want to have the wedding before I start to show, and wanted to ask if you'll make the cake, Bethany. Besides, I'm not sure things can get much crazier than they've already been."

Suzanne laughs. "Just wait until your babies arrive. Life can always get more insane, especially with twins."

"Plus, one of them is going to be slipping out of his diapers all the time," Jennifer adds. "I read that Kirenai boys go in and out of their resting state from the moment they're born."

Her mate, Nazhin, adds, "That's why Kirenai males are so involved with child rearing."

He's the only one at the table with horns, claws, and a tail. His massive wings are currently retracted into his back, or he'd take up three seats. Jennifer says he can also look human, but she prefers his Khargal form, so that's how he appears most of the time, thanks to their unique circumstances when they formed a mate bond.

Tazhio shrugs and says, "I'm always ready for crazy."

Tamara beams at him with a radiance I've never seen on her before, and I realize all my sisters are glowing with happiness. *Do I look the same when I'm with Izhima?* The feeling of contentment is indescribable when we're together. Maybe we should make our relationship official, too. My producers would go gaga over a big alien wedding—and all the food that goes with it. I sit up straighter at the thought. "Let's make it a quadruple event!"

"Hold on." Suzanne raises both hands in front of her. "Kiozhi and I are mated, but that doesn't mean I want to get married. I swore I'd never do that again."

I pout my lip. Leave it to our big sis to be a party pooper. "What's the big deal? You're already bound for life. Marriage is just a piece of paper."

"It's not just a piece of paper. It's the principle of the thing. I'm a free woman and intend to stay that way." She loops one arm through Kiozhi's, as if he's making the stand with her.

He looks at her with adoration and nods. "My love is true with or without paper."

I open my mouth to whine again when Jennifer pipes up. "I'm game. How about if Suzanne is our Maid of Honor? That way, she's still part of things."

Izhima returns and sits beside me, taking my hand. "What'd I miss?"

I bite my lip, realizing we never spoke about getting married. *Too late to turn back now.* I lift our clasped hands to my chest. "Izhima, will you marry me?"

He glances around the table and chuckles. "I'm guessing this is another of your impromptu decisions?"

"It absolutely is!" agrees Suzanne.

"Marriage is the logical next step," I insist.

He kisses the backs of my knuckles. "We're already married in the eyes of my people."

"I know, but—"

"So it's logical to bind myself to you in your tradition, as well."

"You tease." I meet his dark blue eyes with a grin. "Did I mention we're also making the cake?"

Izhima chuckles. "You humans and your cake."

"It's the most important meal of the day." I repeat our private joke with a wink.

He smirks back and squeezes my hand.

"We need a date and a venue," says Jennifer. "I bet the captain would let us hold it on the observation deck. We do have free cruise privileges for life."

Tamara claps her hands in delight. "Do you think Emily and Becca would be our flower girls?"

At eighteen, I think Suzanne's twin daughters are a bit old to be flower girls, but I swallow my argument when Suzanne says, "Of course they will. And I can see to the flower arrangements. Kiozhi bought me a greenhouse on Alkavar III."

Her mate claps Tazhio on the shoulder. "I get to be your wingman for the wedding, right?"

Tazhio laughs. "I think you mean Best Man. And yes, Tamara suggested I ask you."

"Shouldn't the groom be the best man at his own wedding?" Izhima tilts his head in obvious confusion.

My sisters and I burst out laughing, and I lean over to hug my mate. "A Best Man is the groom's best friend or brother who stands with the groom during the ceremony. He also helps with wedding planning."

Kiozhi rubs his forehead. "Why do humans have so many confusing terms?"

Nazhin leans forward, his silvery eyes catching the light from the centerpiece on the table. "I don't have a brother, but it would honor me to have Kiozhi—or any of you—as my Best Man."

"From what I've read about human customs, the four of us will now be brothers-in-law," Tazhio adds with a grin. "I like big families."

Kiozhi's mouth curves into a slow grin. "I've always dreamed of having a brother." He gives Tazhio a solid punch in the arm. "This'll be fun."

"Then it's all settled." I raise my stemmed glass of *Lensoran* bubbly. "Congratulations to the happy couples."

Around the table, seven more glasses raise in reply. "Congratulations to us!"

20

BETHANY

I turn a full circle and look at myself in the mirror one last time. My wedding dress is a sleek, cream-colored material that clings to my curves in all the right places, lifting and accentuating my figure with flattering ease. The patterns Tamara embroidered on the bodice sparkle with crystals matching those in my bouquet.

Behind me in the mirror, Tamara and Jennifer are also getting ready, their dresses equally stunning. Jennifer's gown has a nebulous bit of tech circling the hemline that makes it look like she's floating on a cloud of stars, and Tamara's is made of gossamer lace that makes her look like an angel.

Our stateroom is right next to the lift that will take us to the *Romantasy's* observation deck. Captain Zhanuzh was not only willing, but seemed overjoyed to allow us to hold the wedding—or weddings, as it were—on board. I think it might have something to do with the free publicity the cruise line will get on Earth with the broadcast, because as I suspected, my producers jumped at the chance to televise the event.

My sisters balked at first, but I begged for the sake of my show, and they came around. For the zillionth time that day, I'm warmed by the knowledge that I have the best family in the world. I meet Tamara's gaze in the mirror and she smiles, her eyes dancing with excitement.

Suzanne hands out our bouquets—a mix of Earth flowers and exotic blooms from each of the groom's matrilineal home planets. My cascade of pink, yellow, and orange flowers is tied with a delicate white ribbon and bedecked with sparkling crystals that glimmer in the light. I lift it to my nose and inhale deeply, loving the subtle, almost caramel scent of the petals.

"Are we ready?" Suzanne asks. Her Maid of Honor dress is a slinky, midnight-blue gown that looks like it was cut and sewn directly from a piece of the night sky.

"We're ready," says Tamara, fastening Beanie's leash. The chihuahua has been fitted into a doggie tux and carries a small pillow on his back like a saddle. Six wedding rings glint atop the rich black velvet.

Jennifer and I nod, and we file out into the corridor. Mom, Dad, and Suzanne's twins are waiting for us beside the lift. Emily and Becca are wearing silver flapper-style dresses and pillbox hats woven with ribbons and flowers to match their baskets. At eighteen, they're not little girls anymore, but I think they look adorable all the same. Mom wears a black and white A-line dress that matches Dad's tux. She smiles at us proudly, eyes glistening with emotion.

Dad's hands clench and unclench as he looks at each of us, face stern, but eyes full of love. "I'm not ready to give you all up at once."

"Dad, you promised not to make us cry," says Tamara, her voice thicker than usual.

My throat feels tight, too, and I reach up to adjust his bow tie. His pure white hair is combed neatly over his bald spot, and he even shaved for us, his jowls a bit reddened from razor burn. "You clean up nice, Dad."

"Thanks for not making me wear some new-fangled space suit, kiddo." He's looking warily at Jennifer's hem of stars as he leads us into the lift. He and Mom are still getting used to the thought of aliens for in-laws.

"You all look so pretty," sighs Emily, a dreamy look in her eyes.

"Don't get any ideas," Suzanne chides. "You're too young to get married."

"Mom," Becca rolls her eyes, but before she can add more, the lift doors open and we're greeted by the thrum of the orchestra playing from a floating balcony to one side of the dome.

"Hush, everyone. We're on." Suzanne strolls from the lift.

The girls follow a minute after holding Beanie's leash. The little dog prances ahead of them with his nose haughtily in the air, as if he's the reason for this entire event.

The path down the center of the observation deck is swathed in a shimmering fabric with tiny silver crystals dotting the edges. Lavender and blue lights twinkle through the dome overhead—a nebula Jennifer chose specifically for the ceremony. I have no doubt she's set up instruments to gather data at this very moment.

Thinking of instruments, I quickly search the deck for my camera crew. They'd better be ready to roll. My producer, Sean, is in charge, and it wouldn't be the first time he's fucked something up. Relieved when I spot a cameraman at the end of an aisle, I take a deep breath and step off the lift, taking my spot between Mom and Dad. They're walking us down the aisle together, with

Tamara and Jennifer flanking them and me in the middle.

Dad squeezes my elbow. "Ready, kiddo?"

Catching my sister's gazes, I smile and nod. The music swells, shifting into a traditional wedding march, and I take my first step down the aisle. Over two hundred friends and family sit watching in the pews to either side, and our grooms wait for us on a platform at the far end.

I feel Izhima's eyes riveted on me as I walk. He's dressed in traditional Vatosangan wedding garb—a burnt umber robe with a high collar open at the front to reveal the gold embroidery on his shirt. The love shining in his eyes makes my knees feel weak. I smile back, feeling like the most beautiful being in the universe at this moment.

Next to him, Nazhin is in human form for the ceremony, wearing maroon pants and an asymmetrical tunic, while Tazhio is dressed in a black flight suit with a silver belt. At the far end of the lineup, Kiozhi stands proudly wearing a tux and cummerbund made of fabric to match Suzanne's dress. They might not be taking vows today, but we all know they are as bound together as the rest of us.

Before I step onto the platform, Dad takes my hand and leans close to kiss me on the cheek. "Be happy," he whispers.

My eyes burn as I try to reconcile my conflicting emotions. "Love you, Dad."

Turning to face the platform, I take Izhima's extended hand. The moment he smiles at me, all conflict inside me melts away. His wide, earnest expression makes me feel like I'm the only person in the room.

"You look good enough to eat," he murmurs.

"I was thinking the same thing," I murmur back. Between the lapels of his ceremonial robe, his tight shirt emphasizes his amazing six-pack. My gaze drops lower to the bulge beneath his belt. Damn, my man is hot.

The sound of a small gong draws my attention back to the ceremony. Captain Zhanuzh steps forward, his blue spines sleeked back and his white captain's uniform crisply pressed. He offered to look human today for the cameras, but Sean and I agreed that much of the appeal is in the event's alienness. The captain's mandibles click twice before he begins to speak. "Today, these six people will enter a bond of marriage to one another in the eyes of the Confederation, Earth, and the Universe…"

The ceremony is brief, honoring each of our cultures. Tazhio speaks his vows to Tamara in Hypawan, stroking her fingers and kissing the tips one at a time between phrases. Jennifer and Nazhin recite their pledges in English, short and to the point. And Izhima weaves flowers from his mother's planet into my hair as he promises to honor our everlasting love.

When the captain announces we may kiss, I loop both arms around Izhima's neck. "Welcome to the first day of the rest of our lives."

He drags me against his chest, kissing me so soundly, my head spins. Then I realize the orchestra has begun playing a strange, upbeat combination of strings and synthesizers.

"What's this?" I ask, exchanging a confused look with Jennifer.

"It is a traditional wedding song from Alkavar III," Tazhio says. "Kiozhi might not be getting married, but we thought we'd include a tradition from his home planet, too. Dancing!"

Kiozhi is already leading Suzanne to a cleared area near the orchestra. Izhima takes my hand to follow, with Tamara and Jennifer right behind us. We form a circle, and Izhima leads me through the steps. Soon we're gliding across the floor in a series of dips and twirls that leave me breathless. But it's Kiozhi and

Suzanne who are the center of attention, spinning and striking poses in a display that would put professional dancers to shame.

When the song ends, everyone claps and cheers, joining us on the dance floor for another round. I don't think I've ever seen my sisters so happy or felt so joyful myself.

Soon, it's time for what I consider the crowning event of any wedding—the cake. The four-tiered confection is a replica of the *Romantasy* iced in blue, with tiny, multi-colored planet cakes making orbits around the ship via some sort of alien tech that lets them hover in place. This cake is the kickoff for Izhima's and my new show, *Cosmic Cake Creations*. I'm not sure how Izhima and I are going to top it as a showstopper for the rest of our show's episodes, but I'm not worrying about that now.

I verify the cameraman is in place before we each catch one of the floating, cupcake-sized planets. The one I hold is frosted white with sparkling pink sprinkles, and Izhima's is a deep purple with black crackled lines over the surface. I grin wickedly at him. "You know what comes next."

His face is somber. "Is it truly a tradition?"

"Absolutely." I lift my cake to his mouth. Sean didn't want us to do the cake smash, but I think it will make

Izhima and I feel like a genuine couple for the viewers instead of some unreal fairy tale. "Open up."

In the next breath, we're both smeared in cake, and the guests are cheering. I barely have time to wipe my face before he pulls me in for a kiss. Vanilla, butter, and a slight hint of almond flavor mingles between us as Izhima licks the frosting from my lips. Completely unscripted, he turns to the camera and winks. "Delicious!"

I poke him in the ribs with a grin. "I knew you were a showboat at heart."

He smirks and dips in for another kiss. I return it with all my heart, thrilled I get to spend the rest of my life with my alien chef.

EPILOGUE

IZHIMA

I hug Bethany close to my side and look around the set of *Cosmic Cake Creations*. After the wedding, the captain of the *Romantasy* all but insisted we use one of the ship's kitchens—a fully functioning one—for Bethany's cooking show. The cruise line has had record ticket sales since the wedding aired on Earth, and they even funded a remodel to include appliances from Earth. The only piece of obviously alien hardware is a basic replicator model behind the central counter where we'll be cooking. It's surrounded by flashing, multi-colored lights Bethany's producer, Sean, insists give it "that alien flair" viewers expect. I don't particularly like Sean —he treats everyone around him like garbage—but I try to be civil to him for Bethany's sake.

"I hope we bought enough *kazhitu*," Bethany says, chewing the pinky nail of one hand.

We've filmed several episodes, and the show became an instant hit not only on Earth, but on several other planets as well. A spot in our tasting audience sells for almost as much as it costs to produce the episode, and the waiting list is already more than a year out.

I squeeze her tighter. "That's what the replicator is for. Stop worrying, it's going to be great. And you look amazing, by the way."

She's wearing a vibrant burgundy blouse with large white buttons, and her auburn hair is lustrous in the lights from the camera crew several feet away. She smiles up at me. "Thank you." Running one palm down the front of my chest over the white chef's coat, she says, "But nobody's looking at me. You're the star of this show. Thank you for co-hosting with me."

It doesn't seem to bother her that the nearly all-female audience tends to only have eyes for me, but just to be certain they know I'm taken, I pull her against me and give her a lingering kiss. There is an audible sigh from the women in the audience.

When the kiss ends, we're both a little breathless, and I wish I could spirit her off to our cabin instead of having to keep things acceptable in front of the cameras.

Arms still looped over my shoulders, Bethany looks up at me, her face positively glowing. "What was that for?"

"I'm happy to be part of your dream."

A clatter behind us makes her pull away. "Oh, I think they're here!"

I turn and look past the camera crew toward the big double doors where Sean is entering with his usual entourage of attendees. Bethany's not normally this excited to see her producer, but she rushes over to meet him. I wipe the scowl from my features and move to my position behind the counter. It's better if she deals with him alone.

Along one edge of the counter sit jars and packages of fresh food we had shipped from my home planet, so I take a moment to double check what's there. Today we'll be making something humans call Bundt cake. We've baked several test batches, and Bethany seems pleased with the results.

I look back up to see my mate accompanying a small gray alien toward me. "Izhima, I'd like you to meet Chef Ulan. She's a judge for the Nebula Chef awards."

My mouth drops open. I know who Chef Ulan is. Her work is legendary. I reach out to shake her hand, feeling a little lightheaded before I realize the gesture is completely human. "It's an honor to meet you."

Luckily, Chef Ulan takes the handshake in stride. "The honor is mine," she replies. "I've been following your show since it premiered, and I must say, I'm very impressed with your technique. That, and how adorable you two are on screen together."

Sean moves in close beside her, all puffed up. "Izhima is a fantastic chef. I'm glad I discovered him and put this show together to demonstrate how our cultures can meld."

I narrow my gaze at the annoying human. "I think you mean to say you're thankful Bethany thought up and pitched you the concept. If it wasn't for her, you wouldn't have a show right now."

Sean's face falls, and he looks like he's about to say something, but Bethany cuts him off. "But we do have a show, and it's an amazing success because we all work together. Let's not forget that."

He holds up his hands in surrender. "Yes, well. I'm sure the chef's going to love today's episode. Why don't we get started?"

Chef Ulan dismisses Sean without a glance his way and joins the audience, while a clearly flustered Sean returns to his seat behind the camera crew. I lean close to Bethany. "How'd you manage to get Ulan on the show?"

"I have my ways," she says with a wink. "Seriously, she really is a fan. I'm pretty sure you're a shoo-in for that Nebula star. Now stop grinning like that. We're about to begin."

I can't help myself. I pull her against me for a kiss that gets a standing ovation from the audience.

Dear ARC Reader,

I hope you enjoyed Bethany and Izhima's story and the wrap-up for the voyage on the *Romantasy*. This set of books was a challenge for me to write, both because of the first person point of view and because I made all the sisters' stories happen at the same time. Thanks for sticking with me as I grew my writing skills.

If you're craving a little more from the Bloom sisters, **join my VIP Club for a bonus epilogue** in Jennifer's point of view and a quick jaunt back to the Singing Planet!

https://www.tamsinley.com/romantasy-bonus

Thanks for reading!
XOXO,
Tamsin

P.S. If you didn't read the previous books in the series, I invite you to join the other Bloom sisters on their adventures. Here's a link to where it all started:

http://www.tamsinley.com/tazhio

GLOSSARY

Ahen - an opiate-like drug.

Ayabe - slightly astringent fermented leaves humans might think resembles cole slaw.

Amai wood - a rich golden brown wood sought after for its buttery texture and sweet scent. The resin is used as an aphrodisiac on the planet Hy.

Bacca - a game that resembles frisbee golf.

Bareshi - brilliant one.

Burendo - a Kirenai who excels at shapeshifting and is able to not only assume the form of other species, but coloration as well.

Damma - the Kirenai word for mother.

Fogarian - aliens with red hair and sideburns who live on a rocky, mountainous planet.

G'nax - a species that uses light to communicate attraction and arousal. They also have a symbiotic relationship with an eight-legged insectoid.

Hage - bald, wide-eyed alien that looks much like the iconic alien humans have circulated.

Happa trees - blue fronds resembling palms.

Hypawa - species with magma colored eyes.

ICC - Integrated Circuit Chip - an embedded chip that is an alien version of a holographic smart phone

Ijin'en - four legged herd animal raised for meat and well known for its stupidity.

Iki'i - empathic power.

Irn - a unit of measure. One planetary rotation around the Kirenai's sun.

Itoshi - beloved. Term of endearment.

Jiro - a unit of measure equivalent to approximately two Earth hours.

K'ogai - the town near the palace on Kirenai Prime.

Kazhitu - nuts that look like sticky buns when baked. High in sugar, buttery and fruity.

Khargal - a gray, horned alien with stone-like skin and wings from the planet Duras ;)

Khensei - a toxin that causes Kirenai to denature into their resting state.

Kikajiru - my distracting one - a term of endearment.

Kirenai Prime - the Kirenai home planet. Purple and blue with swirling white clouds.

Klen - aliens who communicate via scent.

Kuro - a type of bitter, very black tea.

Kuzara - shit, damn, fuck.

Kryillian death swarm - tiny insectoid creatures that can kill a man within seconds by sucking his blood.

Lensoran bubbly - alien champagne.

Lonala moth - fragile insect native to Hypawa.

Malila flowers - fragrant, night-blooming flowers popular in conservatories across the galaxy.

Lukulio - purple worm-like insects usually consumed while alive.

Matrix/cellular matrix - the term for a Kirenai's cellular mass.

Nezumi - a small downy animal with a stumpy tail and floppy ears found on most space stations.

Nilgawood - a tree used to make resin.

Oritsu - An expression of awe.

Popotan - the plant used to line ship interiors that provides oxygen, recycles water, is highly resistant to radiation, and can regenerate itself if damaged.

Qalqan - a species known for their healers. Good bedside manners due to their resistance to emotional fluctuation.

Resting state - a Kirenai's amorphous shape, like nakedness to humans, it is shown only to family or trusted friends.

Senburu - a galactic conglomeration of merchants who oppose the emperor's rule. Individual members are called *Senbur*.

Sheegr - a hyper-sexual, weasel-like species native to the Singing Planet.

Sireta Prime - a popular party planet.

Sowain - tastes like chicken!

Supo cloth - smart fabric for clothing that doesn't need buttons or zippers.

Tekina - the galactic word for human.

Teozhisa - a cart to carry people.

Tolonovone - a device that creates lighted markings on the skin. Used by G'naxians as part of their mating rituals.

Ukimi ice - beloved dessert with cool, spicy flavor like sweet mint.

Urru - purple egg-sized fruits from the Singing Planet that taste like cantaloupe.

Vatosangan - a species with alabaster skin and blue or green hair who tend to be stocky or rounded. Planet is called Vatosang.

Zhinku weed - common in the popotan fields.

Zhikegi - morning stimulant drink.

Kirenai are an all-male species of shapeshifters with a natural form (resting state) like an amoeba who usually assume a bipedal shape to interact with other species. Until the discovery of humans, Kirenai required a permanent pair-bond with a female of another species to produce offspring. All Kirenai traits are dominant and located on the Y chromosome; male offspring are fully Kirenai, while female offspring are fully of the mother's species.

Birth rates have been historically low, and over the ages, the population has dwindled. Human females are exceptionally receptive to impregnation, and do not require formation of a pair-bond to conceive, which has made Earth a target for black market slave traders who deal in "breeders." The Emperor is making attempts to protect the population.

Regardless of the shape a Kirenai's matrix is in, he cannot change his skin or hair color. The most common color is blue, although hues range anywhere from mint green to lavender. Rare individuals, called *burendo*, can vary coloration outside this range. Kirenai blood is clear or slightly milky unless infected, when it grows murky to almost solid white.

All Kirenai have empathic abilities called *Iki'i* which make them capable of reading emotion and desire, and also enables them to identify individuals within their own species regardless of shape. This is the only Kirenai trait sometimes passed on to female progeny. The ability also makes the species consummate lovers because they can take actions and form attributes their partner finds most appealing. Bonded mates assume a permanent form pleasing to their mates; rarely can they force themselves into an alternate shape after bonding.

The average Kirenai life-span is approximately eight hundred human years. When a pair-bond is formed, a Kirenai passes a small genetic market to his mate that mitigates the aging process, giving the mate a lifespan to match his own.

Qalqan – A pink, lizard-like race who are innately skilled at medicine. They have more than two genders and change genders as they age, which makes reproduction rather complex. It also means means they rarely pair-bond with Kirenai. In addition, their emotions are hard to understand for others and unreadable by Kirenai *iki'i*.

Hypawa – A race with large, expressive eyes, smooth luminescent skin, and luscious hair on their heads and eyelashes; considered by many to be the most beautiful race in the galaxy. Their origin is a mystery - even their supposed world of origin doesn't seem to be their homeworld. Their economy is dependent on tourism and entertainment.

G'nax – A spiny, bug-like race that can breathe a variety of atmospheres. Biologically they are inclined to be traders and have senses that let them navigate through hyperspace. They use light to communicate attraction and arousal. The females have a symbiotic relationship with an eight-legged insectoid which secretes dew used to feed G'naxian infants.

Khargal – A horned, gray-skinned race that can enter a hybernating state where their body becomes stonelike. The number of horns indicates the amount of royal blood in them. Honor is more important to them than anything. They have wings and claws and resemble gargoyles of Earth mythology. Their planet of origin is a barren world that has two moons and is known for having some unusual ore deposits and relatively few life forms.

Fogarian – A burly, thick-skinned race with crimson hair, claws, and fangs. They come from a high-gravity planet rich in crystalline gemstones and excel at digging. The females usually bear litters of two to four offspring, and are favored mates for Kirenai. Fogarians tend to be very straightforward and keep their promises, even if it means death.

Vatosangan – A small, slight race with alabaster skin, rounded features, and blue to black hair. As the most common race to pair-bond with Kirenai, some say they actually control the galactic empire behind the scenes. They seek any alliance, technology, or advantage that will benefit them, and their current government is a meritocracy.

Klen – A green-skinned humanoid race with eyes on extendable stalks. Their tongues can act as prehensile limbs, and they have the ability to withstand a wide range of temperatures. They are a race of scavengers and can modify some of their bodily secretions to become various useful substances.

Hage – Short, bald, gray-skinned aliens with large heads. They were the first to make contact with humans. Though their scrawny frame doesn't suggest it, they are addicted to the pleasures of taking nutrition, and their cuisine is spectacular. A past war obliterated their homeworld, and they now live scattered among the other races, usually employed in a service capacity.

Sheeghr – Not advanced enough to be admitted to the Galactic Confederation. A matriarchal, ferret-like race native to the Singing Planet. Known for hypersexuality, the females maintain a constant state of pregnancy to ward off a native parasite called a Gloor. Any female who refuses or who cannot get pregnant is killed. The males determine rank based on the size and color of their phalluses.

Human – New members the Galactic Confederation. This bipedal race has not yet homogenized into a single language, culture or appearance. The species has skin tones that vary between black and alabaster, with shades of brown in between. The females are capable of reproducing with many other species throughout the galaxy, and have become a target for illegal slave trading.

INTERGALACTIC DATING AGENCY

Looking for more out of this world romance? Your local Intergalactic Dating Agency can help! These strong, smart, sexy aliens are on the prowl for mates, and humans like you are exactly what they're after. Jump in with Book 1 of any standalone trilogy from our crew of rock star SFR authors and make steamy first contact! Warning: abductions may or may not be included!

Grab more hunky alien action here:

http://romancingthealien.com

ALSO BY TAMSIN LEY

SCI-FI ROMANCE

Galactic Pirate Brides series

Kirenai Fated Mates (Intergalactic Dating Agency) series

Khargals of Duras

FANTASY ROMANCE

Mates for Monsters series

PARANORMAL ROMANCE

Alaska Alphas series

AUDIOBOOKS

BOX SETS

BOOKS IN GERMAN

Gefährten für Monster

Alphas in Alaska

POST APOCALYPTIC SCI-FI written as Tam Linsey

Botanicaust series

ABOUT THE AUTHOR

Once upon a time I thought I wanted to be a biomedical engineer, but experimenting on lab rats doesn't always lead to happy endings. Now I blend my nerdy infatuation of science with character-driven romance and guaranteed happily-ever-afters. My monsters always find their mates, with feisty heroines, tortured heroes, and all the steamy trouble they can handle. I promise my stories will never leave you hanging (although you may still crave more!)

When I'm not writing, I'll be in the garden or the kitchen, exploring Alaska with my husband, or preparing for the zombie apocalypse. I also enjoy crocheting while binge watching Netflix, playing video games, and enjoying family time during our weekly D&D session.

Interested in more about me? Join my VIP Club and get free books, notices, and other cool stuff!

www.tamsinley.com